SCRATCH

A novel by

Paul Jones 2022 Copyright

THIS STORY IS A WORK OF FICTION.

IT OFFERS NO THEORIES ABOUT ANY EVENTS OF THE TIME,

NOR SHOULD ITS CONTENTS FORM THE BASIS OF ANY.

" You've got something. George Talley had something too - once."

"He can have it again," I said, "if he plays his cards right."

"If that's what it takes," she said, "you can scratch him off right now."

- The Lady in the Lake by Raymond Chandler

'It is not fitting for a fool to live in luxury…' Proverbs 19:10

CHAPTER ONE

The decade known as 'the Sixties' was like any other party where food and drink are plentiful. It began as revel and ended as riot. It began with music and laughter and ended with screaming, fighting and crying. It was a complex decade, but a few fragments of history – not in any specific order - can sum up the flavour of those years.

The decade began in 1960 with the misplaced hope in youth represented by the election of US President John F Kennedy. It ended in 1970, with the break-up of Britain's most successful export company, the Beatles. They had defined the decade, so everyone said. Also in 1970, that other most emblematic British company, Rolls Royce, nearly went bankrupt.

Social upheaval almost became the norm in the late sixties. But it was a healthy decade. Everyone was living longer – they needed to, to pay off their hire purchase agreements. Everyone felt immortal, especially the rock and pop musicians who behaved as though they were, and consequently started going down like cannon fodder. The American comedian Lenny Bruce told his audiences that narcotics were not dangerous but friendly. In 1966, the drugs showed their gratitude by killing him.

In 1964, a Conservative government which had protected itself from scandal by covering up a homosexual relationship between a Tory peer and violent psychopath Ronnie Kray was thrown out of office. It was replaced by a socialist government which covered up the same scandal in order to protect Labour MP Tom Driberg, who was almost certainly compromised by Soviet intelligence. Conservative Ted Heath was elected Prime Minister of the UK in 1970 and he inherited the chaos of the times. But sadly for the country, he had nothing to offer but his best. This story takes place in the exact mid-point of that decade: June, midsummer of 1965. The cranes of London's docks had been bowed before the coffin of Churchill earlier in that year. The Beatles, on the back of the success of *A Hard Day's Night* were filming *Help!* The country was moving from black and white to colour. The world of monochrome went first to Technicolor and then to psychedelia. Aspirations became dreams and then hallucinations.

In England, another rock group The Who – allegedly representing *My Generation* - expressed their contempt for comfortable materialistic society, by ending each gig by smashing up their instruments. But they could afford to replace them as they were paid unbelievably comforting sums of money.

Wilson 'Scratch' Garner, was one of the older men who would have been happy to assist them in the destruction – preferably before they started playing. Born in Peoria, Illinois, he had moved to London in 1964, where he drifted into that emerging demi-monde where celebrities, sporting personalities and criminals mixed and made common cause. He was seen in the East End at the clubs belonging to the vicious Kray brothers and in the South where the equally barbarous Richardsons ruled. And of course, in Central London's Soho, which was turf to be quarrelled over by various parties, including the police.

The details of Scratch Garner's flight from the United States are, like most of the details of his life, uncertain. But some few are not. Criminals may lie with abandon, but the facts of their activities are usually better recorded by the authorities. We know that he was born in May 1923, making him 42 at this time. We know as much about his father as he did, which is next to nothing. He may have been Scottish or of Scottish descent. Garner probably parted company with his Danish-American mother as soon as he was too old and too big for her to carry him back home every time he ran away. We know that he was in jail in America twice. Once for stealing some money and once for knifing someone who had stolen some of *his* money. (Possibly, it was the same money.) But birth, for people like Garner, is like the first drink at an orgy. After that, everything gets a little hazy. His passport was undoubtedly false. Even his documents told tales.

He arrived in the Smoke around September 1964. One thing is sure and that is that he must have brought some money with him. It is equally certain that this money was being missed by the original owners who may have made forceful enquiries concerning its whereabouts. Clearly, it wasn't a fortune, but it was enough to allow him to set up in a modest flat and buy a small car. It was also enough to allow him to frequent particular types of pubs and clubs where he sought 'contacts' and 'opportunities' of a vague kind.

Cube novelists, whose characters are little more than police descriptions, would have noted that he weighed about 190 pounds and was six feet tall. To call him ugly would have been to miss the point. It is irrelevant with men. A man can resemble Caliban and be attractive. His savage looks did him no harm with some women, especially as they associated it with the glamour of danger - which effect he was quick to encourage with engaging tales. These tales were, like dreams, constantly in a state of flux. There were women in abundance at the Grey Cat Casino in Soho that evening. This being the sixties, the clothes were still beautiful.

Now the Grey Cat was not a top-of-the-range casino. You wouldn't see Princess Margaret or Peter O'Toole there. But at the same time, it wasn't full of Chinese greengrocers handing over the deeds of their shops to a card-sharp wearing an eyepatch. It was plush and glamorous enough, as mid-range places always are. Mid-range people try harder, wear their best clothes and look like they want to get on in life. No wonder then that the Grey Cat was based at a point equidistant between the rich West End and seedy Soho.

Garner was suited and booted, as the saying goes. He knew there were celebrities there, although he wasn't too sure of their names. You can always tell when famous people are in the room. It has the same effect as a strong gust of wind parting a field of wheat.

The big, busty blonde who was talking very loudly in the middle of a group of admirers, was someone he knew. It was the actress, Diana Dors. She had been to America. She was wearing a tight black cocktail frock. If she had anything in her wardrobe that wasn't tight, it was probably a kaftan.

'So I said to him, listen darling, if that's your bloody attitude then you can stick it where the doctors daren't operate...'

He looked at her. She stopped talking and held his glance for a few seconds before turning away. She looked to the side, which meant she wasn't sure. He felt the urge to do something to attract her attention.

Between him and the buxom starlet was a roulette table. He placed some chips to show that he was betting on one third of the board.

'All twelve,' he said, making a wave of dismissal to the numbers. His voice was low and indistinct, and often had to be accompanied by gestures to force through his meaning.

Miss Dors wasn't looking at him now. She was talking to another young man. But he could tell she could see him out of the corner of her eye. Garner was an expert at this sort of look. He had spent all his life being carefully but surreptitiously scrutinised, especially as a young boy in department stores.

The wheel span and he won. Number ten. She turned again and made a face of sarcastic amazement. Yes, she had been watching him. He motioned to the croupier to leave the bet where it was.

'Again,' he said.

He had bet twenty pounds originally. He could not afford to bet twenty pounds, but he had nothing to lose. If the numbers were against him he could impress her by shrugging, as if it was only money. And if he won, well, he was better off.

The wheel spun and he won again. Number three.

The croupier looked at him and he felt a curious conflict of emotions: confidence and unease, as if he were not in control of his movements. He gave Diana a tight look – almost but not quite a smile - and placed his entire winnings - £180 - on number thirteen. He couldn't believe what he was doing. He had won enough to live on for a season and he was about to blow it to impress a woman who could have used the money to tip the milkman. Everybody in the casino went quiet and was watching him. Garner liked the attention. So far, anyway.

The croupier, who happened to be Yugoslavian, mouthed his cod French and tossed in the ball. It rattled and jumped for an agonisingly long time while the Fates argued over it. Then it stopped. Thirteen. Everyone at the table applauded and Diana gave him a light-hearted, deferential nod.

He grabbed hold of himself, pulled the chips in and placed a fraction of it on the black diamond. It won. After a few more cautious but successful bets, he had £8,200. This was more money than he had ever stolen in his life. And by some miracle, he had come by it honestly. By another miracle, he managed to stop. He was not the sort of man to offer a gratuity to the house. (Not because he was mean – he was American and knew how to tip - but because he simply wouldn't have thought of such an obvious nicety.) He picked up his winnings without thanking anyone and went to cash them in. He was trying to think of a smart remark to say to the admiring crowd, but his wit failed him. Later on, it occurred to him that he could have said something like,

'How about that? Now the Brits are bailing out the Yanks. I always knew you'd be back.'

But it didn't matter now. It didn't matter anyway to Garner. He didn't want the fame, just the money. The clientele, having applauded politely, stared at him blankly, with resentment, as if he were an intruder. As though he were taking their money. But without a doubt, he would have many friends before the evening was over.

CHAPTER TWO

Garner sat at the cocktail bar and ordered a big scotch with more ice than the poor bartender had in his little bucket. It is not as easy as you might think to gauge his emotional state. Naturally, he felt good. But he was a man of entitlement and had a high sense of self-approval. Already, the demons were whispering in his ear that he was a naturally lucky man and would be again. (What on earth was there in his life up to now to justify this belief?) They were softening him up for the next step, which was to tell him how clever he had been.

'Lucky night for you, my friend,' said a voice behind him. It was an easy, confident London voice. It was the voice of a man who wasn't afraid to talk to strangers because he could expect to be liked.

Garner turned to see the man who was speaking to him. He wouldn't have known the Prime Minister of Britain, but he was a sporting man and he knew Freddie Mills. Mills had been a boxer, better known for his ferocious determination than his scientific precision. He was now a fading celebrity – still sometimes on TV, but not as often - and a nightclub owner, recognised and liked in the shadowlands of the capital. Craggy faces seemed to be in with men at the moment, like miniskirts with women. Perhaps they suggested the cachet of working-class origins. Mills had one. It was the face of a man who could laugh at himself even while on the ground, which Mills had been on many occasions.

Mills introduced himself and his companion, Lenny Dessau, a portly, imposing man in his fifties with darting eyes full of subtext, intrigue and suspicion, which were at odds with his easy conversation.

'Pleased to meet you,' said Dessau. 'Pleased to meet you!' He shook Garner's hand ferociously with a wrestler's grip. But he had never been a wrestler. He had the look of a man who got other people to do all the heavy lifting in life. His suit would have cost more than Garner's car.

'They call me Lucky. Lucky Lenny. But you're the lucky one tonight Mr...'

'Garner. Wilson Garner. But people call me Scratch.'

'Any friend of Freddie Mills,' said Dessau. Garner was now a friend of Freddie Mills, it would appear.

'Let's have a drink,' said Dessau.

Garner tried to insist, but Dessau insisted harder in his turn. Mills let them do all the insisting. Garner realised that now that he could afford to buy drinks, he would probably never have to again. Well, not for the foreseeable future. Garner had scotch, as there was no Bourbon in England. Not where he went anyway.

'I bet you can't stand our warm English beer,' said Mills. And they all laughed.

'It's an acquired taste,' replied Garner. 'I don't plan to acquire it. This must be the only country in the world where the tea is colder than the beer.'

And they all laughed again. Garner would find it very easy to make people laugh – again, for the foreseeable future.

They chatted amicably. Mills explained that Dessau was a bookie, to which Dessau objected,

'Please! Turf accountant. Allow me my dignity, Mr Mills.' And this was good for another round of laughs.

Dessau kept looking around to see if anyone had heard what he did, as though they were alone instead of in a crowded venue. He was obviously one of those curious people – they are more common than you think – who could talk about their personal business in a loud voice in a public place, and then object when others overheard them. The conversation naturally drifted off into horses and the track. This kept them going for a while.

'Over here on business?' asked Mills.

'Let's say I'm looking for opportunities,' said Garner.

'Oh, you'll find plenty of those over here,' said Dessau.

'Definitely,' said Mills. 'London is buzzing at the moment. There's an energy here. You can feel it in the air. You'll meet a lot of interesting people.'

Dessau agreed enthusiastically. Both men produced business cards. Dessau's was embossed and shiny; Mills' was plain and tatty.

'Come to the club sometime,' urged Mills.

Dessau thought this needed some elaboration.

'Freddie's a nightclub owner now. Best place in London. Can't move there for celebrities - and other names. Isn't that right, Freddie?'

Freddie could hardly disagree.

'You want to meet people, my spot is *the* spot,' he said.

'Maybe I will,' said Garner. 'Do the Beatles go there?'

'Not recently. We had the Swinging Blue Jeans in the other week. They're doin' OK.'

Garner had obviously never heard of them. He wouldn't have wanted to meet the Beatles very much either. But it would have said something about the club if they had been regulars.

'Maybe I will come at that,' he said again.

'And come to the races too,' said Dessau. 'And the doggies. I'm well known there. Bring some of your luck with you.'

Garner was pretty sure that Dessau meant 'bring some of your money and lose it', but he assured both men that he would not be a stranger.

'His club used to be a Chinese restaurant,' said Dessau, nodding knowingly, as though this were an important fact. Everything Dessau said was delivered as if it were crammed full of significance, like a bad actor playing Harold Pinter. He would have made a crackerjack tour guide at the Tower of London. Garner glanced at Mills' card.

The Nightspot. – (Well, no-one could say the name was misleading.)
Proprietors F. Mills and A. Ho
Soho.

'Will the blonde lady be there?'

'Diana? I know Diana. She's all right. Great star. Great personality. Got a heart as big as a house.'

Garner gave his trademark tight half-smile.

'I've got a house as big as a heart at the moment. But I plan to move soon.'

More laughter.

'He knows everyone, our Freddie,' added Dessau, just to make sure he was part of the action. Then he looked furtively round again, as though the place might be bugged.

'Certainly do,' said Mills. They drank up and Mills bought another round. Garner had hoped that he might get an introduction on the spot, but when he looked around, Diana had gone. She was clearly doing what most celebrities did, especially those who weren't quite so hot as previously. She moved around from place to place, getting photographed, being seen, kissing other celebrities and then moving on to the next venue. In one or another of those places, sooner or later, she would meet someone useful. A producer, perhaps, or an advertising executive. Or a bank manager who'd had a few too many. ('You'll never guess who I gave an overdraft to last night.')

Or perhaps, she had wanted to be the centre of attention and Scratch had stolen her thunder.

'I must be going soon,' said Dessau, banging his empty glass on the counter. 'It has been a gentleman's pleasure and a pleasure, gentlemen, as always. I must go home to my wife and family. I'm getting too old for this nocturnal world. The older you are, the more you appreciate family. Young people don't know that. Things are crazy these days. See me doing the Twist? Blimey! As I said to Freddie just now, you're over the hill at thirty these days. Am I right?'

Mills agreed that he was certainly right, although he was clearly having difficulty remembering that Dessau had said it.

'You said it, Lenny,' said Mills. 'You certainly said it.'

Both men refused the offer of Garner's drinks. His credit was good now. They didn't need the drinks back just yet.

'I'll get you a taxi,' said Freddie, which may have told Garner, if he was paying attention, something about the nature of the relationship between his two new friends.

Garner was happy he had met them. Mills would know people and Dessau would know the money. Somewhere in between might be a chance for Garner. People like Garner were always looking for something like a chance or an opening or an opportunity. His ambitions never got any more specific than that.

'If you're anywhere near Kilburn, I can offer you a ride,' said Garner.

'Well, that is most obliging of you, sir. Most obliging. Didn't I say he looked a most congenial sort, Freddie?'

Freddie could only agree that he had certainly said it, he just wasn't sure when. Garner shook hands with him and promised to show his face at the Nightspot soon. Both men headed out into the dark. It had been raining lightly but it was a warm June night. Garner's Ford Popular was parked nearby. In those days, you could park easily. He was angry that a man like Dessau would see his shoddy little motor, but he could say with honesty that he would be changing it soon.

'Where we headed?' asked Garner once they were both in the car.

'Hampstead,' said Dessau.

Garner just knew that Hampstead was nowhere near Kilburn. But he was happy to take the bookie home. Dessau was clearly a man of some significance and Garner wanted to prove that he was a most obliging fellow.

CHAPTER THREE

In the car, they chatted occasionally. Dessau talked about Mills a lot. 'Wonderful feller. Great boxer in his day. Absolute whirlwind. Dynamite. Then he went on telly. Family man, though. Let's be fair, let's be fair. Lovely guy. Good all-round egg.'
And so forth.
Garner didn't doubt it. Dessau was a man who liked and expected to be listened to. Garner tried to interrupt a few times, just to get the ball back across the net. But Lucky Lenny never seemed to come to the end of his sentences. There were commas and pauses and hyphens – but no full stops. (Or periods, as Garner would say.) Everything he said seemed to remind him of something else which urgently needed to be said. Dessau was one of those people who didn't need an interlocutor, just a separate body so that he didn't look like a lunatic talking to himself. He should have been a ventriloquist, thought Garner.
The streets of London were quiet in the sixties and Hampstead wasn't so far away. Dessau had occasionally interrupted himself to give directions and they soon pulled up in front of an expensive looking Georgian house. The windows were all dark. If anyone else lived with Dessau, they were long in bed. The same with all the other houses. They had watched *The Epilogue*, had their cocoa and retired. This was a respectable neighbourhood.
'Here we are, safe and sound, home and hearth,' chanted Dessau. He heaved himself – oof! - out of the car and gave it of his opinion once more that Garner was a most obliging fellow.

Garner could see another car, a Rover, parked across the street. Two men got out and walked across the road. Dessau was not so self-absorbed that he couldn't notice danger. He probably looked for it in the bathroom.

'Stay in the car,' he said as he bent down to talk through the window. In a loud voice, he said, 'Thank you so much for the lift, my friend.' Then he dipped his hand quickly into his pocket and drew out a large brown, unmarked envelope. He tossed it on the passenger seat.

'Give me that back next time you see me,' he whispered. 'But don't mention it to Freddie.'

Then he walked up to his front door. The house had a big front garden, and it was quite a way to that door. The men went after him. Garner sank into the driving seat just far enough that he could watch and hear. The sight of a near-200lb man trying to crouch down in a Ford Popular must have had something of the ridiculous about it. But thank God, there was nobody to see it. And Garner was not a man to worry about the aesthetics of dignity when survival was at issue. He had switched off the engine when they arrived, as he had guessed that Dessau would take a long time to wind up his rambling conversation. Now he switched it on very slowly, as if doing it slowly would stop people hearing it.

Garner got a good look at the two men. One of them – the smaller of the two - wore a trilby. People were still wearing hats in the sixties. Oddly enough, it was the hippies who kept the practice alive. But these two guys were definitely not hippies. Perhaps the hat-wearer liked watching Humphrey Bogart movies, although it was too warm for a mac. He had the hat pulled down over his eyes. The other - the bigger of the two - appeared to have been a boxer at some time. Garner knew the gait and the look. He had kept his head in one piece by taking a few dives in the third round before things got rough (and before he couldn't get any more fights). The smaller one in front was the one who was going to do the talking.

'Lucky Len!' he said. 'Well, well, fancy running into you round here!'

'What do you mean, running into me? I live here. And you've been waiting for me by the look of things.'

'All right, all right,' said the hat-wearer. 'No need to take offence. I was just having a look. Nice area this is. I'm thinking of moving in round here.'

'You've picked a bloody funny time to go house-hunting,' said Dessau. 'Anyway, you couldn't afford a coal-bunker in this neighbourhood.'

'Oh, you are a snob, Lenny,' said the spokesman. His accomplice guffawed. 'Now there's no need for any unpleasantness. You know what we want.'

'Freddie wants it,' said the bigger man. He probably wasn't supposed to have said that.

'Let me do the talking,' said the trilby to the boxer. 'You just stand there and look desirable. Now, Lenny...where is it?'

Lenny said that he didn't know what they were talking about, which was a silly response really.

'Don't make us search you, Lenny...I mean Mr Dessau. Where are my manners?'

He'd been waiting all his life for a situation like this so he could try out his gangster dialogue. He even smoothed down Dessau's jacket lapels.

Then he tipped his hat up. Garner would know him again. His smooth face looked like plastic. Of course, he was far away and it was dark. Perhaps it was just the contrast with the boxer, whose face looked like the surface of a shelling range.

'I don't know what you're talking about,' insisted Dessau.

'Spell it out for him,' he said to the boxer.

'We want the list and the Chinese box, Lenny,' said the boxer.

'I don't have either,' said Dessau.

At this point Garner remembered that minding your own business was a virtue where he came from. He decided that Dessau was not so lucky after all and that maybe he wasn't someone whose society he needed to cultivate. He could see Dessau looking at him, thinking that maybe because any friend of Freddie was a friend of his that Garner might pitch in and assist. Perhaps he had thought that he knew Garner quite well after one evening. He was getting to know him a bit better now.

Garner did not know exactly whether he was a coward or not. No situation had ever tested the issue. The matter was probably completely beside the point. He preserved himself as though that were his ordained profession. To do otherwise would have been a dereliction of a sacred job specification. Self-preservation was the nearest Garner had ever got to a calling.

Dessau and the men were about thirty feet away from him, up the long garden path to the house, so Garner had no fear that they would be able to chase or catch him, although they might be able to see his registration plate.

The men, following Dessau's helpless gaze looked at Garner now. Perhaps at first they had thought he was just a cab driver. Now he was a witness. Dessau, sensing a distraction, did something really stupid. He was probably not in the habit of making stupid mistakes and this may have been his first one. But it was also his last. He hit the boxer. It was a good punch for a portly, middle-aged man who was out of condition. (He must have been a lot harder in his youth.) The boxer – who had obviously never shone in his profession – fell to the floor. But the punch wasn't enough to knock him out, so it wasn't, effectively, of any use at all, except to enrage the man.

Garner had his head down and could just see over the dashboard as he gunned the car to make his getaway. He heard the smaller man shout,

'No, not that – put it away, no!'

And then he heard the gunshot – which was very loud at 2.00am in a quiet residential area. As he sped away, he straightened up and could see in the rear-view mirror, that the two men were running across the road to their car. He wondered if they might follow him, but it was unlikely. Their car was pointing in the other direction - and these two men weren't going to do any fancy choreography involving three-point turns. They headed off pretty fast. Maybe the smaller man had had the brains to realise that a screeching of brakes would not have helped the situation.

Next to Garner, on the seat of the car, was the large envelope. Whatever was in it was enough to send people out with guns looking for it. And guns were not readily used in the UK, not like they were in America. Someone wanted it very badly.

So that was the end of Lucky Lenny Dessau. His luck turned out to be the same as everyone else's. It stopped at the grave.

CHAPTER FOUR

When Garner got back to his drab flat in Kilburn, he was almost afraid to get out of the car. Imaginary police sirens sounded in his head. A nationwide manhunt was already underway in his fevered mind. His face would be on television. A neighbour of Dessau with artistic skills and an eidetic memory had peeped through the curtains and had managed to draw a lightning sketch of the man police wished to interview. They were looking for an American man in his forties with a Chicago accent and a small scar on his left wrist, possibly caused by an accident with a can-opener. The neighbour, also an expert in phonetics, could tell from the way Garner had said 'goodnight' that he had once lived at 14 Delaware Street in Peoria and had been engaged to a Mexican woman called Chica.

His hands were shaking. He had seen violence before, but he had never witnessed a murder. He was not nearly as blasé about such things as he had supposed.

When he finally got his wobbly legs out of the car door, all he could hear was the silence of the unfashionable sideroad where he lived. How he had managed to drive home was a mystery. Only now was the shock hitting him. He crossed the road with nervous quickness, expecting a convoy of police cars at any minute, and let himself in.

Garner's flat was rented, obviously. It seemed to be much harder to get a self-contained apartment in London than in the US. It was one third of what had been a very large Edwardian house at one time.

The estate agent had said that the flat had 'all modern conveniences'. However, he had clearly thought that this phrase included things which were not inside the flat, like the laundrette across the road. Sadly, there was no 24-hour liquor store nearby. There was probably no such thing in England. This was a shame. He desperately needed a stiff one and he had nothing in the house. This angered his American soul. He had a demand and the money to back it up. He expected the supply to be available.

Once inside, he sank down in one of the kitchen chairs and put the envelope on the breakfast table. He looked at it as he tried to catch his breath. Naturally, he was curious about the contents. That was an easy problem to solve: all he had to do was open it. But he just stared at it. He may have wondered whether, if he opened it, it would change his circumstances. But his circumstances had changed now anyway. And, he reminded himself, minding your own business was a virtue where he came from.

He took out the wad of money and cheque which combined made up the £8,200 he had won that night. He had a good stare at that too. It was a much more enjoyable and rewarding stare. He may have asked himself if he needed any more of the opportunity which the contents of this mysterious envelope would provide. He could now afford to leave this dump, he thought. He was on the up, without a doubt. Why reach for more? He had won a small fortune and been a witness to a pointless slaying. That was a good argument for laying low for a while. He had been lucky and then unlucky. Just like Lenny Dessau. It seemed to him that this was typical of the sort of pattern he had come to expect in his life.

He stared at the various items on the table. What was he to make of this puzzle? He had won enough money to ward off his troubles and then stumbled into some more. One thing however was clear: whatever was in the envelope, Dessau didn't need it anymore.

He stared some more at the envelope. He was tantalised by a mystery which was easily solved. If he wanted to find out what was in it, he just had to reach for it. But he didn't: he just looked at it.

Photographs? People would play a heavy game in a case of blackmail. But most blackmail victims were likely to be weak. *Nobody would blackmail me,* he said, threateningly, to the whole world. He thought it unlikely that a man like Dessau would let anyone get one over on him. Of course, Dessau might have been blackmailing someone else. No, unlikely. It's a filthy game, blackmail. A certain type of person specialises in it, he guessed. Dessau hadn't looked like someone that low. (Like many people of doubtful morality, Garner had to have other, lower lifeforms to feel superior to.)

He slid the envelope towards himself. He remembered the story of the million-pound note. (They had done that at school, although Garner had not handed in the assignments and had played dice on the back row with the bad boys.) But he remembered the story. He did not remember the story of Pandora's Box because he had never heard of it.

All he had to do was open it.

But then what? What horrors would be unleashed upon the world if he did? More importantly, what terrors would he bring down upon himself?

This was a far more important consideration. If he just handed it back unopened...but to whom? Freddie? And was Freddie, Freddie Mills? There were plenty of Freddies in London. Don't show it to Freddie, Dessau had said. Some friendship those two had.

Once he opened that envelope, he was involved in something – and he probably wouldn't be able to get out. Maybe someone would send an armed party wearing trilbies to find him.

The £8200 should have made him think that he didn't need any more accidental adventures. He had been lucky enough for one lifetime. But it didn't. It had, after due consideration of the alternatives, the opposite effect. It made him think that his miraculous evening was the beginning of something great. Something greater, even. Something he had been owed all his miserable life and was now going to be delivered upon. More than that, an adventure story in which he was the hero. This was only the beginning.

He got up and went to the kitchen drawer. In the drawer was one fork, one spoon and one knife. The knife was too blunt for cutting anything tougher than a fried egg, but it could be used to open an envelope. He replied to his own scruples by saying, *Open the damn thing.* So he stuck the knife in the side and slit open the envelope. He pulled out the contents. They consisted of two pieces of paper. Both pieces contained a list of what appeared to be bank account numbers and Christian names.

He stared at the lists. Bank account numbers, all different. No bank names, no sort codes. And just the first names. No surnames. Some of the names sounded foreign. The bank numbers were probably from all over Europe. There was a Jacques and a Helmut, in among all the Geoffs and Davids. There were one or two female names too. All false, no doubt. Small amounts salted away in different places and adding up to a fortune, most likely.

The surnames and the bank names would be in the Chinese box. That was an easy deduction. He took out the card Freddie had given him. He had them both: Freddie's and Lenny's. He used the gas plate in the kitchen to burn Lenny's. That was a good start: already he was destroying evidence. Then he used the gas to light a cigarette. He looked again at Freddie's card.

The Nightspot

Soho

Proprietors: F Mills and A. Ho.

The Chinese Box. Ho seemed to be a Chinese name. Maybe.

He let the lists fall onto the table and stared at them again. They would be completely useless but dangerous to him now that he knew about them. Unless he could find the other half, that is. Did that mean the Chinese box? Was the other list really in the Chinese Box? Or was it just a valueless and much-loved heirloom belonging to someone's grey-haired old mother which Lenny had taken as collateral for an unpaid betting debt? Of course, he could destroy the list. But that would be a bad move if he had to trade it for his life later on.

A lot of thoughts went through his tired, alcohol fuddled mind, although he was not usually a man given to introspection. The one thought which was the most important: namely, that he might be out of his depth, somehow got lost in the confused mix.

He folded up the lists. Needless to say, he didn't have any reading books in his flat. But he did have an AA book of road maps, so he placed the lists in there. A better hiding place would be needed later, but no-one would come for them tonight. He felt better now that he was back in his own place. The sirens in his mind faded away.

He took off his tie, jacket and shoes and lay on the bed. He slept instantly, although the events of the night whirled around in plangent, jagged fragments inside his head. Garner was not used to bad nights. He had no conscience to keep himself awake and no dependents to worry about. And, ironically, this was the first time in a long age that he had had no money troubles.

On June 15th, Leonard Marcus Dessau was cremated at Golders Green Crematorium. There were not as many people there as might have been expected. Clearly, Dessau's friendships were as superficial and transitory as the ones he had fleetingly enjoyed with Garner and Mills. Dessau had known a lot of people, but they obviously now felt that he was no longer useful to them and had stayed away. Garner did not go, of course. Neither did Mills. Neither did Diana Dors, if she had known him. Neither did a couple of hundred other people to whom Dessau had been introduced by friends of friends or who had done business with him. He was lucky to have his family there. Of course, family was very important to him. He had always said so.

CHAPTER FIVE

Garner was astounded to find, when he awoke, that he had taken more care of the (presumably) useless lists than he had of his winnings. The cheque and cash were lying on the table where he had left them. He had slept late. Now he needed a good breakfast and to open a bank account. In England in the 1960s, it was easier to organise the latter than the former.

He had nothing in the house, so he searched hard for a greasy spoon that wasn't too contemptuous of basic hygiene standards. There he ate a breakfast more hearty than healthy. Then he found a local branch of Martins bank. The experience surprised him: it had taken him over a week to get his telephone installed, but he was out in half an hour with the promise of a temporary cheque book in the post that day. He only hoped he wouldn't have to move before it arrived. He also managed to get a haircut. He found a traditional barber who did three styles: Tony Curtis, National Service and Ringworm.

Now, there was one more thing, which he had been putting off. He bought one of Britain's famously imaginative newspapers. There was a report in the afternoon edition about the slaying of a gangland bookie. There were no facts in the piece that he did not know – although there were a few which seemed to have been invented. The piece was written by the paper's star crime reporter, Jess Hammond. He was already famous for writing the best-seller, *James Dean: Slain by the Mob*. He had also, the blurb reminded the reader, been the first reporter in Britain to expose the links between Teddy Boys and their KGB handlers.

Garner was gratified, however, to learn that there had been no witnesses to the killing. (If you're a criminal, the best thing is no witnesses. But several witnesses are better than one because they all contradict each other.) Neighbours had heard a car – or possibly two cars – speeding off. But no descriptions. No-one had actually *seen* anything. The police urged anyone with more information to come forward. The usual pre-printed slogans.

Originally, Garner had wanted to go to the nightclub to make contacts and get to know celebrities. Wealthy as he was now, that wasn't so urgent. But he had to talk to Freddie Mills for three reasons.

Firstly, he wanted to find out what Mills knew about the situation. After all, Mills knew for sure that he had given a ride to Lucky Lenny. Mills probably wouldn't go blabbing to the police; but he was not a gangster: he didn't live by the code of Omerta. Secondly, his first plan was not necessarily out of court. He had money now and that was always the best time to make new friends. Thirdly, he wanted to meet Diana Dors again. Mills was his only conduit for all these things. And so, as was usual in his life, he went with intentions but no real plan. Events would decide for him.

Back at the flat, he got out the list from the book of maps. Where to hide it? It couldn't stay here, that was for sure. He'd seen a spy film once in which the CIA had searched a room so thoroughly that they'd taken all the wallpaper off. That would be an improvement in his flat, but he couldn't leave the list here. Someone determined enough would have all the plumbing out.

One idea would be to send it to himself by mail. Registered mail, perhaps. That was an idea that worked once, but he couldn't do that every day. To do it a few times would tempt fate. If it didn't arrive on time, he would think all sorts of things. And it would look suspicious too. In the end, it was the only idea he had. *Hi, me again. Just sending the same list to myself. No, no reason. I'm just lonely. Makes me think I have friends who send me stuff.*

He went out to the Post Office and joined a miraculously orderly line. He sent the list to himself, registered. Then he bought a few provisions – including the bottle of scotch which he should have had to hand last night - and a local paper which might have accommodation ads in it. On returning home, he rested for a while and smoked. He also managed to find a radio station that wasn't playing the Beatles all the time. Then he dozed off. When he awoke, it was time to get ready and go to the club.

CHAPTER SIX

When he arrived at The Nightspot, he was expected. The cashier took his details but waved away his entrance fee and ushered him inside. Like all nightclubs of the early 60s, the Nightspot had a foot in two eras. There was live music with a female singer. There were semi-acoustic guitars, a stand-up bass and a drummer. Pop songs were sung in the jazz fashion and jazz standards were altered slightly so that guests could do the twist to them. Lightshows of the time were rudimentary and usually centred around a glitter ball in the ceiling.

Garner took stock of the place. The club was good enough, but there was nothing unique about it. It was probably a good place to be, but it was never going to be *the* place to be. You could have a good time here, but you could buy a bottle of hooch and a radio and have a good time on your garage roof. Celebrities would come to the Nightspot briefly as a favour to Freddie before moving on somewhere with more photographers. (And more people to be photographed with.) Those who stayed were either people on the way up but not quite there yet, or those on the way down who had never quite touched the sun before their wings started to melt.

The club boasted a decent bar. There was also a stage which was too small. Later on, a band nobody had ever heard of would come out, cram themselves onto it and sing all the wrong songs in the wrong tempo.

'Scratch, my old mate. How are you?' said Mills. People made long-term friends easily round here, it seemed. Especially if they were in the lucky lane. Garner had only just been served at the bar when Freddie appeared behind him. They shook hands.

'Good to see you, mate. Got everything you want?'

Garner was puzzled: Mills seemed very chipper.

'You do know what happened to Lucky Len, don't you?'

'Yeah. Read about it in the papers. Terrible thing. Nice bloke, Lenny.'

Mills didn't seem to want to question Garner about what had happened. But Garner was keen to offer his explanation.

'He told me to drop him off at the end of his road. He must have known people were waiting for him and wanted to keep me out of it. I never saw anything.'

'Yeah, that must have been it,' replied Mills in a distracted way. 'He knew some bad characters, so they say. But he wouldn't want to get you involved. That makes sense. Like I say, he was a nice bloke.'

Mills was only too delighted to see things Garner's way.

'I must say you're taking your friend's loss very well.'

No doubt Mills had to keep up appearances. After all, he was at work now and playing the role of a professional host.

'He was all right, Lucky, but a bit full of himself. I didn't know him that well.'

'You didn't? He gave me the impression you grew up together.'

'No, not at all. You know how it is with some people: they take a shine to you without your permission. Rich people do it a lot. Especially if they're one-way conversationalists like Lucky Len. No, I wasn't especially close to him. Met him a few times, nothing more.'

Obviously, there was more to this, but Garner couldn't guess what. Money maybe, which was his default explanation for the mysteries of the soul and the contradictions in people's ways. Perhaps Mills was just cultivating people. Was he in some kind of financial trouble? Maybe the club was failing. Garner made a note to ask around. But he couldn't ask around until he knew the right names. Mills, for the moment, was his only door to this kind of society. Not that Scratch was concerned about Mills' difficulties, but he wanted to get his story straight.

'Hey, listen Freddie. You're a straight up and down kind of guy. I need to say something. It's like this: I've got a couple of deals bubbling under at the moment.'

'Good stuff. Glad to hear it. I like a nice business deal. We should talk sometime: we've got things in common... I mean a proper talk. Away from all the bustle.'

'Sure. What I mean is ...I wouldn't want any er...interference just now. You know...bad publicity.'

Mills nodded with easy understanding.

'Sure, no problem. I understand, mate.'

'I didn't know Len. I was nothing to do with him. I just gave him a ride home.'

'Don't you worry, Scratch, my old chum,' said Mills taking his arm. 'Schtum's the word. Schtum.'

Mills waved an expansive hand gesture across the entire club.

'We're all friends here. We mind our business but we look after business, if you know what I mean. Now let's have that drink you offered me.'

Garner ordered the drinks and then Mills insisted they were on the house. What a crazy world it was when you had money. Everything was free.

'Good health,' said Garner.

'Cheers...Oh, and about that other matter...'

'Other matter?'

'Miss Dors. She's just arrived.'

Garner looked, and there she was. She didn't look at him but was smiling to the whole world. She seemed to know and want to kiss everybody. Her teeth were miraculous for an Englishwoman. Garner imagined her sitting on the hood of a Rolls Royce. Then he imagined more.

'Will you introduce me?'

'My pleasure. But remember one thing about our Di. She either loves you or she loathes you. And she'll decide very quickly.'

Diana Dors had enjoyed stardom at a young age in the fifties. She had even been offered opportunities in Hollywood. But things had not gone to plan and she was currently in the process of re-relocating back to London. Her marriage was on the rocks too. She would have been about thirty-four now. Still very beautiful, but busty was verging on buxom with corpulence sensing an opportunity.

But if she was on her way down for the moment, the tiny, saucy little creature with her was definitely on the up. This was Barbara 'Babs' Windsor, the actress who had starred in *Carry on Spying* the previous year. She was wearing a bright red spangly dress with headband and handbag to match. The outfit suited her. She was a spangly sort of person.

She, in turn, was accompanied by her new husband, Ronnie Knight. A small craggy – there was that word again – man with a history of trouble in the criminal spots of East London. This little tableau was the sixties encapsulated: sportsmen, celebrities and criminals came from the same streets and frequented the same shady places. Sometimes, they got up to the same mischief; fame and notoriety fusing together and becoming indistinguishable in the dark corners of the newly affluent and morally negotiable world.

Windsor was never beautiful, but she was bubbly and loveable – and she was especially loved by the camera. She had successfully marketed the notion that she had large breasts - which in truth she did not. Knight was a routine cockney geezer, telling tales of how he knew Larry the Leg down South who was a mate of Big Chester of the Chobney Gang who did that blag on the Securicor van in Croydon – or some such stuff. Enough of it was true to mark him down as a villain; but enough of it was false to identify him as a talker.

Garner was introduced to the crowd by Mills who 'loved them and left them' to get acquainted.

'Well,' said Diana, 'it's the Gambler. This is Pasteboard Pete, the Terror of the Riverboats. Hope you haven't come to blow your ill-gotten gains.'

She did a confidential stage whisper to Babs Windsor.

'This man is a big shot from the States. He was down the Grey Cat the other night, throwing his money about on the big wheel. They reckon he killed a man in Tombstone.'

'Oooh! Did you win? You can blow your ill-gotten gains on us, if you like,' said Barbara, giggling. She looked like the sort of person who thought that wine came in two types: red and white.

'Sure, I won: I always win.'

'Really?' drawled Diana. She could see that his suit told a different tale. There was nothing wrong with it; it just wasn't a winner's suit. Garner wore suits well and he had never needed to have one made. (This was just as well, given his erratic history of earning.) Off the peg stuff fitted him snugly, but it doesn't pass for Savile Row no matter how good the fit. And Di Dors could spot a faker in an instant. She'd fallen in love with enough of them. And there were plenty more in show business.

Garner shook hands with Knight and they had some drinks.

'So, how's the film industry?' asked Garner, looking at Diana.

It was a magnificent faux pas. It would have been the right question to ask Barbara Windsor but not Diana. Things had gone wrong for Diana Stateside, and the situation was precarious. Barbara came to the rescue. She spoke as if the question had been addressed to her.

'It's all up and down,' she said. 'This year I'm doing well. The next year, I'll spend six months sitting by the phone. Same for everyone.'

This diplomatic intervention smoothed things over, but Garner felt the moment slipping.

'How's the gambling industry?' asked Knight.

'Same for me I suppose. One minute you can be in the chips, the next minute you're on the skids again.'

Garner could feel the weight of his leaden words. Then Diana spoke.

'I'm having a party next weekend. A week on Saturday. Why don't you come?'

There was little warmth in her voice and she was looking at him in a curious way.

'Thanks, I'd like that.'

She took out a card from her purse and wrote her address on it.

'There'll be some card players there. There's going to be a game. You might be interested.'

'I'll look forward to it.'

'Bring a girl, if you like,' added Diana, saucily. And then they were gone. They had seen some people over there, but it was very nice to have met him.

Garner stood alone for a while. He went and stood at the bar, where he would feel less embarrassed. Then he saw Ruby.

Ruby Irons was what used to be called a cigarette girl. She had a tray of cigarettes and matches and was dressed like a chorus girl in basque, fishnets and a twinkling rhinestone headband. Her wages were mainly made up from the tips which lustful, drunken men gave to her when they bought her overpriced wares. Ruby would have sold a lot of cigarettes. She probably sold them to men who didn't smoke.

'Cigarettes, sir?' said the little brunette. She smiled at him.

It was probably the only innocent smile Garner would ever come close to. He bought a packet of cigarettes from her, paid for them and put an extra ten-shilling note in her costume.

'That's just for you.'

She thanked him and made to leave.

'Hey, where are you going?'

'I'm not to fraternise with the customers.'

She had trouble with the word 'fraternise'.

'That kind of defeats the whole object of the get-up, doesn't it?'

She laughed.

'Yes, I suppose so. But I am at work.'

'I'm not a customer. I'm a friend of the management, so it seems.'

'Are you American?'

'What gave me away?'

She laughed nervously.

'Are you an oil tycoon?'

'Do I sound like I'm from Texas? I'm from Chicago.'

Garner wondered what kind of naivety would think an oil tycoon would come to this garage. Suddenly, he was seized with a strange delusion of being mature, wise, experienced and glamorous.

'Chicago!? My goodness. Are you a gangster?'

'What if I was? Would you make a run for it?'

She laughed.

'I'm sure you're not.'

'No, I'm not a gangster, I'm a gambler. This week I won fifteen grand at the Grey Cat casino. I've met a lot of gangsters though. Part of life, where I come from.'

'Gosh! £15,000? How did you win?'

'Poker game,' he said. His eyes never left hers.

'You must be very clever.'

'Yeah, sure. It's no mug's game.'

He tapped his head.

'You've got to have it up here. A memory for cards and the ability to read faces.'

She was impressed. Then she looked furtively around.

'I'd better go or I'll get told off.'

But she stayed.

'Don't tell me, you're a singer and you got this job in the hope they'll audition you.'

'No, I'm just a cigarette girl. But I can sing.'

He thought for a moment she was going to say that she sang in a church choir, but she didn't. Ruby looked longingly at the musical combo which had just started its set on the small stage. The female singer, wearing a long, silvery evening gown, was making mincemeat of a jazzed-up version of *Wooden Heart*. Her voice was all power and no subtlety. Garner thought she was good.

'I wish I was a real singer,' said Ruby, turning back to Garner. 'I'd love to meet famous people.'

'You meet plenty here, don't you?'

'I mean to know them - as an equal. They don't really notice you when you're staff. I must go.'

'My name is Wilson Garner, but everyone calls me Scratch.'

'That's an interesting name. I'm Ruby.'

'You'd better get back to work. I wouldn't want to get you into trouble,' he said.

He nearly added the crude and obvious rider, 'At least not in that way', but by the time he had fetched it up out of his collection of burlesque rejoinders, she had gone. This was just as well, really.

Garner wandered around for a while, trying to make conversation with strangers, which is not as easy in England as it is in America. He asked people how they were. It was like asking how much money they made. Eventually, he caught up with Mills again.

'Enjoying yourself?'

'Sure.'

'How d'you like the band?'

'I think they're getting the upper hand.'

Mills laughed easily.

'How d'you make out with Miss Dors?'

'I don't know. I don't think she liked me. She decided quickly, like you said. But she invited me to a party.'

'Did she now? That's show business, all right. People don't like you but they want to suck up to you. You're getting to be quite a celebrity.'

'Will you be there?'

'Of course. Everyone who used to be anyone will be at Diana's bash.'

Mills rejected a drink. This was his job, he explained, and he had to pace himself. He wasn't a big drinker anyway.

'Still keep in shape?'

'Of course. You never know who's gonna take a swing at you in this life.'

They both laughed. This man Mills was very easy to like.

'Especially in your business, I'd guess.'

'Well, most of my guests are good people. But you only need one lunatic to shoot you. Same as driving. Doesn't matter how careful or good you are, it's how drunk or stupid the bloke coming the other way is.'

Garner agreed. He'd been the other guy often enough to know.

'There is one more person I'd like to meet.'

'Name it, my friend. Say the word.'

Garner fetched out the business card Mills had given him.

'Your business partner, Mr Ho.'

'Andy? He's not here. He does the back-office stuff. Admin and the like. Ordering stuff. He can't work the rooms like you and I can.'

'You mean he's not a people person like us?'

'Exactly. Come round tomorrow morning – late on, towards lunch. We'll be there then.'

Mills excused himself. It was strange the way he had readily agreed to Garner's request. He hadn't wanted to know why Garner wanted to meet Mr Ho. Perhaps he knew. Or perhaps he really did want to introduce him to the business side of things. Perhaps he wanted Garner to make…you know, a little investment in a thriving Soho hotspot. Well, he was entitled to ask, just as Garner was entitled to tell him to drop dead.

Garner drank his drink and winked at Ruby from across the dance floor. She smiled nervously and then turned away. He borrowed pen and paper from the barman, tipped him generously and asked him to give her a note.

The note said, *I can't call you, so you'll have to call me.* Then he added his number.

'Ruby? Sure, I'll see she gets it.'

'What's her second name?'

'Oh, I couldn't tell you that, sir,' said the man expectantly.

'I gave you a pound, you greedy bastard. What's her second name?'

'Irons, sir. Ruby Irons.'

'Thank you so much. You got a big future in bar work.'.

'Not at all, sir.'

Garner glanced at the band. The singer was hammering out the old standard *Lover, Come Back to Me* in a voice that was guaranteed to keep him away.

Garner had forgotten about Diana Dors now, but he would still go to her party. And he might take Ruby. Well, she had said he could.

He left the club. It was a warm night. A handful of night owls were milling about outside too. They were all in a festive mood, as if the experience of trying to find a taxi was a holiday adventure. British people loved the summer and couldn't get enough of it, mainly because there wasn't enough of it. Summer had its compensations for Garner, but generally he preferred the dark. The longer and colder the nights, the better. But the best thing about summer was that it was a long way from Christmas. Not that Garner hated Christmas. His hates, like his likes, his loves and other enthusiasms, were very few, But Christmas had an unfathomable effect upon him. There was no avoiding it and he felt uncomfortable when surrounded by it. It was the hardest time to be left alone. It was a time of unavoidable good feeling. He found this intrusive somewhat. Of course, you could encounter intrusive bonhomie in the summer too, but it was neither compulsory nor so widespread. But apart from Christmas, the cold and the dark were best. Garner had never felt nostalgic in his life before, but he found himself thinking fondly of those freezing Chicago winters, with the sidewalks roped off to stop people being impaled by falling icicles. And everyone wrapped up warm and minding his own business.

CHAPTER SEVEN

Clubs, theatres and schools all look ghostly when they are empty. More so than any fairground haunted house. Any business which is built around a lot of people gives off the wrong impression when you see it deserted. A place can look as if it is struggling, even when it isn't.

Garner arrived about 11.30am and was shown into an office the size of a porter's lift. Mills was there, standing, leaning against the wall. He had a different look on his face from the one he used to greet the guests. Garner had formed the impression that this place was in trouble.

Seated at the cluttered and battered desk was a portly, middle-aged Chinese man who could only be Mr. Andrew Ho, Hong Kong businessman and former actor. At one time, this office must have been the notoriously careless kitchen of the Chinese restaurant that the building once was. Chinatown, in London's central Soho district, was only it its incipient stages then. Mr Ho was probably a pioneer.

Mills arranged some coffee and Garner was offered the only other chair.

'Well,' Mills began, 'here you are at the centre of a pulsating and go-ahead enterprise.'

Garner and Ho gave forced smiles.

'I'd show you around the club but you've already seen what there is to see.'

'You got a good little place here. I like it,' said Garner.

Mr Ho saw his opportunity.

'It has potential,' he said, 'and it makes a good profit. But we could do so much more.'

And there it was. All they needed was a little more investment and this swinging hot-spot would be telling Elvis Presley to wait in the queue along with everyone else.

Did it heck make a profit, thought Garner. They were probably ten minutes away from the street auctions. 'Cash flow problems' was the new buzz phrase to describe imminent bankruptcy. All it needed was an 'injection' from some businessman with an eye for the main chance. Someone who had just won a few thousand pounds on the tables. Somebody lucky who wanted to be luckier. El Dorado was just around the corner, if they could only pay the suppliers who were sitting on the barrels round the back with red invoices clutched in their angry fists. Maybe there was more. Maybe there was protection involved too. Nothing surprised him. Garner had a lively imagination when it came to the myriad forms of trouble that the world could offer. But it had never protected him from them.

'Well, I don't doubt it could use a little investment,' said Garner, and they all laughed. It was a real laugh this time.

'Maybe you'd like to think about it,' said Mr Ho, who seemed more in a hurry than Freddie. Of course, he probably knew the state of the books better than Mills. But money wasn't really the issue.

The place didn't need money – at least not in the long term, if the present financial stresses could be alleviated. It needed ideas. Which is odd really because normally when money is the issue, ideas are all people are prepared to invest. The place lacked flair, which was perhaps not surprising. Mills had grown old in grimy tents and smoky halls full of people who desired only noise, nicotine, booze and blood.

He was trained in the entertainment of wartime austerity, where you provided only the basics. He had had no preparation for satisfying the alluring new dreams of the multi-coloured, plastic post war era. Truly the sixties had taken everyone in Britain by surprise.

Not that Garner would have known this. He had no flair to offer. And in any case, money was the only ingredient whose potency he recognised. To him, money was base, flavouring and yeast.

'I'll be glad to think about it,' said Garner. 'Can I ask a question?'

'Ask away matey, ask away.'

'Do you know what a Chinese box is?'

There was a pause. If they were expecting that question, they made a good job of hiding it.

All three of them looked at the desk. In amongst the pens, paper, rubbers, pencil sharpeners, invoices, family pictures, final demands, coffee cups and assorted bric-a-brac was a little box. It was the sort of thing you could buy in a joke shop or novelty store. Its surface was made of a tessellation of different coloured tablets of wood. You could only open it with the right combination of presses and pushes. No buttons or openings were visible on the surface.

Oh, yes,' said Mr Ho, as he picked up the box. 'An interesting item. You're looking for one of these?'

'Yeah, you might say I have an interest in finding one. It may not be that particular one, but you could say I have an interest in finding one.'

'And me being Chinese, you thought I might be the logical place to start. Well, it's not an unworthy train of thought. Although I do draw your attention to the fact that this one is made in Croydon.'

Mills had gone very quiet. Nobody smiled. Mr Ho looked at the box and then pressed it in a few places. It opened. The box was empty. He handed it to Garner, who examined it, although not with very much analytical inspiration.

'Any more questions?' asked Mr Ho.

'I'm satisfied. Like I said, it's probably not the one I'm looking for.'

'Good, then let's get back to business,' said Ho. 'Namely, the opportunity for a little judicious investment.'

He was going too fast and the urgency showed.

'You mean like investing in the club? Well, sure. It's got potential, like you say. I'll certainly think about it.'

Mills chipped in at last.

'The pay-off would be handsome. This place is a gold mine.'

Garner thought it certainly resembled some kind of pit, but he kept his mouth shut. Protected more by stubbornness, suspicion and self-absorption, rather than any financial acuity, he advised them that he would need a few days to think it over.

'Sure,' said Mills. 'In fact, I'll see you at Diana's next Saturday. You can tell me then.'

This would give Garner a week's thinking space before he made a decision.

Mr Ho frowned. He thought Mills had sabotaged his pitch, when in fact Mills had realised that Ho was forcing the pace: Garner needed more cultivation. Ho stood up and said,

'When shall we three meet again?' He had been an actor once, but the other two didn't get it.

Garner stood up and Mills unglued himself from the wall. They all shook hands. Mr Ho knew *Macbeth* and Mills knew people, but neither of them knew enough to close a deal on the spot. Clearly, from their lack of enthusiasm, they had expected a lot more from the first meeting. Things were obviously difficult for them.

CHAPTER EIGHT

Garner left and went to sort out various errands; then he returned to the flat. This place really was a heap. Now that he was in the chips it seemed to grow worse with each viewing. It had been a useful pied-a-terre when he had first arrived in England, but if he was going to be meeting new people – celebrities like Diana Dors – then he needed a better place to operate from. And a better car.

He bought a paper and read it while eating a pub meal so disgusting in its preparation and niggardly in its portions that it would have shamed a Salvation Army hostel. Nobody at the bar had the nerve to ask him if he had enjoyed the meal and probably no-one cared. In England at this time, you served up filth and people obediently paid and ate it. This was attributed to the post war austerity, even though the war had been over for twenty years. London was the 'swingingest' capital in the world, said Vogue magazine's British editrix, but you couldn't get a decent meal anywhere, except in the places where they served caviar and there were no prices on the menus.

There was very little in the news about Lucky Lenny anymore. Gangland shootings were rare and made the headlines, but obviously no-one much cared if the killers were caught. There was outrage that these things were allowed to happen, but the killing itself was not an outrage. The story was kept on life-support for a while by one or two writers who claimed to be 'insiders' to something. They may have thought that there was a book in it.

Was the IRA involved? asked one columnist, planting nonsense in people's heads and backing it up with circumstantial evidence. Speculation in the sillier newspapers had been the usual custard-pie fight of acronyms: CIA/KGB/IRA/NATO/MI6/MI5 - not to mention the mafia. Eventually the facts were covered in gunk until they all stuck to each other and became an indistinct mass. And then the story was dropped in favour of the next outrage. But it occurred to Garner that he was safe from the police as long as Freddie Mills kept his mouth shut. This meant that Mills had something on him. Of course, he was innocent of any crime, but he didn't want anything to do with the authorities at any time and especially not now. He reckoned that Mills was desperate enough to try to turn the screw. Not that he was a bad or violent man, but he might slip a few hints that they needed to stick together. Mills was everywhere celebrated as a nice guy and a decent sport; but he mixed with disreputable people. And there was no guessing what a desperate man could do if he was days away from financial oblivion and had something on someone who was flush with cash. Of course, Garner had a tendency to judge everyone by himself. He knew how *he* would act in such a circumstance. However, that could be dealt with next weekend.

But for now, there was no knock at the door, no-one hanging about in the street below and no threatening phone calls. The only call came from Ruby who was in a phone box. Her family was too poor to have a telephone. He took the number and called her back. He told her about the party and said he would take her if she wanted to come. Of course she wanted to come, but she would have to see if she could get next

Saturday night off. If he wanted to get in touch with her, he had to leave a message at the Nightspot. That place was becoming an intrusion into his life, and he was naturally a loner, dependent on nobody.

He slept well on Friday night. Back to normal. No dreams.

On Saturday – a week before the party at Diana's - the Royal Mail, one of the few things in Britain that functioned properly, delivered three missives to him. One was the list, which he had sent to himself by registered mail and which he had to sign for. The next was a small parcel from the bank, which contained his chequebook plus a nice letter welcoming him to the privilege of lending the bank his money, and the various penalties for abusing their generosity. The third was a large manilla envelope, not dissimilar to the one Lucky Len had chucked on his passenger seat before meeting his destiny. Now Garner was the recipient of another mystery envelope. He was beginning to feel like some underworld correspondence holding centre. He sat for a long while, trying to pretend he was having an intelligent debate with himself about the pros and cons of opening it. He knew very well he was going to do just that.

As with the first envelope, he followed the ritual of staring at it, pulling it towards himself and then taking the same blunt knife and opening it. Perhaps he was hoping that it would contain the other list, the one with the surnames and the names of the banks. But it didn't. Of course it didn't.

Inside the envelope was a photograph. Not a proper photo, but a clipping from a newspaper. The article attached to it had been cut off. Above the photo was a caption saying, *To the Strongest the Spoils!*

Garner turned it over. On the back, which showed part of an advert for rupture pants, someone had written in ballpoint pen the same sentence as the newspaper rubric: *To the strongest the spoils!*

The photo itself was probably taken from some cheap local rag. It showed what appeared to be some kind of charity event held at a down-at-heel gym, probably in the South or East End of London. Various sporting celebrities were there, plus a few faces who looked quite shady. Many gangsters liked the smell of charity events. Not that they were so stupid as to steal the money but because it was good publicity for them, gleaned from other people's generosity. It is a technique which is well known to media stars these days: raise money from other people and get yourself photographed handing over the cheque to the hospital. He recognised Freddie Mills and Diana Dors. Also Barbara Windsor and Ronnie Knight. There were two other men who seemed like celebrities in the picture as well. They were dressed like exotic professional wrestlers. There was also the obligatory blonde model holding the big cardboard cheque made out to the recipient of their generosity, in this case a children's ward at a local hospital.

In the middle of the gym was a huge barbell; it looked as though some sort of competition was going on. The barbell looked very heavy. Garner doubted if anyone there could have lifted it. Perhaps it was just a comical event – Freddie was a known clown – and no-one was meant to win. The cheque for the money raised was for about £125. The party afterwards must have cost more.

To the Strongest the Spoils. Whose writing was that? Someone was telling him that whoever was the strongest person in that room had the box and the other list? Maybe. But why not just damn well tell him? Why the big mystery? Why the riddle? Was that Mills' writing on the back? Could it be Mr Ho's? *To the strongest the spoils.* It sounded like something a bad actor would practise saying in front of a mirror.

He sat staring at the photo. Some of these characters would be well-known. He could ask anyone about them. The others, maybe not so. Occasionally, he took out the list and stared at it, just for something different to look at. He was a lucky man in his collection of things to stare at. They did not talk to him, or communicate anything, over and above the words typed on the page.

Later on, Garner breakfasted in the usual place. He ordered the 'Big Fry-up' which wouldn't have fed a child in the United States, and sat at a table. The tattooed man who served him his breakfast had a tea towel tucked into the front of his trousers as an apron. It looked as though it had been taken from the used laundry basket in a military hospital. The other customers would have been equally at home in a soup-kitchen. They looked very sad for a bright summer's day. Only the flies were enjoying themselves.

After a few minutes, an old man came and sat down with a bacon sandwich and a mug of tea.

'Hi there,' Garner said, as cheerily as he could manage.

'Morning.'

'You look like a sporting man.'

'Sporting yes, betting no, if that's your game. Whatever it is, mate, I ain't buying.'

'Not at all. I don't want your money, just some local colour. I'm a stranger here. Can you tell me who any of these people are in this picture?'

'I'll have a go,' said the man, adding that his eyes weren't what they were. He pulled a pair of rickety old reading glasses out of his jacket pocket and squinted at the picture. Nothing about him was what it was.

'Well,' he said, eventually, 'you've already marked Freddie Mills and Diana Dors. And Babs Windsor.'

'What about the others?'

'Blimey, it's a grainy photo. Mind you, everything I look at these days is grainy. Especially the wife.'

The man laughed. His teeth looked like the bottom of a coal scuttle.

Garner smiled tightly in encouragement.

'These two look like wrestlers,' he said, helpfully.

'You're not wrong, mate. I think that's...what's his name? Wears a pigtail.'

He took a swig of pale grey tea, to help him think. Then he took a bite of the sandwich. He had mastered the esoteric technique of doing both things while talking at the same time.

'Trademark, you might say,' he continued. 'Oh, what's his name?...'

Garner tried not to scream but the man eventually said, 'Pallo, that's it. Jackie Pallo. And that's his rival. McManus... Mick McManus.'

'That's great,' said Garner, writing the names on the photo. 'Do you recognise anyone else?'

'No. That bloke in the suit by the door – I don't like the look of him. Looks like a wrong 'un.'

'He probably is. Thanks Pops. You've been a great help.'

Garner offered him a pound note and was astonished when the man refused it.

'No, bless you. No need for that. Happy to oblige.'

Never in his life had Garner seen anyone, especially not a poor man, refuse money. These Brits! What could you do with them?

So far, so good. But there were other people who had to be identified as well. Some were in their PT kit. Others, in suits or best frocks were just the audience. He could probably discount them. He was due at Diana Dors' next week. If she could tell him who won or who was the strongest... but what about Miss Dors herself? She was a mighty strong character. Maybe that was what the clue meant. She could tell him so much, if she had a mind to.

After he had finished eating, he returned to the flat for more staring at the picture. All he had was that someone was telling him that the strongest person there was the key. Theoretically, it should be easy: just ask someone who was there.

He looked at the photo again. It was a little piece of the shady world of sport, celebrity and criminality. And there was that wrong 'un in the shadows. Was he the strongest in terms of power? It wasn't one of the Kray twins. He knew what they looked like. He'd drunk a couple of times in their local haunts. He'd seen them photographed as though they were people to look up to. He'd seen them in the papers. If he could find out the identity of that man, he might have the whereabouts of the box and the second list.

As for the first list, he would have to find a safe place for it. Perhaps his bank would be able to look after it. Some kind of safety deposit box. That was a priority. But he was under no financial pressure, even if Mills and Ho were. There was no hurry. The panic over the murder had subsided. The following week would be filled with mundane matters: some new clothes, apartment hunting and a little relaxation. A secure location for the list. Those were his main concerns. And a date with Ruby. Time, for now, was on his side.

CHAPTER NINE

When the next Saturday came round, Garner took a private cab to the party. Firstly, he wasn't too sure that his car wasn't marked by someone. Secondly, he wanted to have a couple of drinks. Not that he was much for social conscience, but he didn't want any trouble with the police just now. Trouble with the police might send him back to America where, without a doubt, more trouble would be waiting.

He picked up Ruby from outside the Nightspot, where she had told her parents she would be working. She hadn't known Garner much more than a week and already she was lying to her family. She was showing great promise.

They made their way to the suburbs north of London where Diana was currently residing. Technically, she was still domiciled in the USA and the house they were going to was probably temporary. She had a husband and a child in the US, but both her marriage and financial status were under great strain. Being in America may have given her some respite from the crippling tax regime which the recently elected Labour government was imposing on anyone it deemed to have earned more than they thought fit for people to have.

They arrived at a salubrious cul-de-sac. They could hear loud music coming from one house which, they assumed, was where the party was. Miss Dors was said to be very religious in private, but nobody was going to be playing the Hallelujah Chorus tonight. Her social gatherings were said to be acquiring a certain notoriety for reasons which do not concern us here.

The front door was a robust affair with black panelled slats and two fake columns made of plaster on either side. Before they could ring the bell, the door was opened by a drunken man in a dinner suit who looked as though he designed cravats for a living. He waved them in majestically and then staggered outside to be majestically sick on the front lawn. Garner and Ruby could not help looking at him. The man pulled himself up with dignity and said,

'You are quite correct to condemn me for my greed. I am ashamed of myself.'

Then he giggled hysterically and went back in for another drink.

Inside the largish lobby the lady herself, in an emerald green dress with a red sash, was holding court to various admirers. One man with a foreign accent that Garner did not recognise, presented her with a bouquet of flowers and said,

'My darling Diana, I will love you for a thousand years.'

'Better give up smoking if you want to pull off that trick, honey,' she replied.

She took the flowers and threw them on the sideboard, where they lay with several other sprays. They would be dead by the end of the evening. So would some of the guests by the look of them. This party would be an all-weekend job without doubt. Nobody would call the police about the disturbance though, or if they did, no-one would come. The local chief constable was probably here. He was probably upstairs being sick in the bath.

Garner took Ruby up to Diana and presented her. It was touch and go that Ruby, the starstruck cinema goer, didn't curtsy.

'Well,' said Diana, 'if it isn't the Gambler.'

'This is Ruby, Miss Dors.'

'Yes, we know each other, don't we? We're old friends,' said Diana, with sincere kindness, patting the young girl's arm. 'You help yourself to anything you want and ask if you can't see it. Enjoy yourself, my love.'

Clearly, it was only pretension that unleashed her waspish tongue. She didn't shoot innocent bystanders.

'What a lovely house!' Ruby stammered.

'Thank you, my dear. It's all down to hard work. You don't get anything in this life by lying flat on your back, do you boys?' she said, winking. She said this to the house and the boys all guffawed.

Ruby was from Strone Road in the East End of London. No display of wealth could ever seem garish to her. Garner took stock of the place. He guessed it was rented. Her home was still in America. Homes were much cheaper there. Was everyone in this damned country either a pauper or living beyond their means?

'Did you think I wouldn't come?' Garner asked Diana.

'Sure, but I never thought you'd bring a girl.'

Everyone guffawed again. The man with the flowers laughed the most, although he had no idea what he was laughing at.

'Well, help yourself to anything you want and don't smash the furniture. It's not paid for,' said Diana.

This got a big laugh, although it was probably true. Then she turned away and they were dismissed. They moved into the main living room which had a well-stocked bar. They took some drinks. Ruby was a useful companion to have as she could identify the famous faces.

'Look! That's Sid James over there,' she said in wonder. If craggy was in, it was in with a vengeance with James, the comic actor. He made Mills and Garner look like girls in a baby lotion commercial.

'And Barbara Windsor. Oh, my goodness,' she exclaimed, 'it's like being on a film set!'

'I've already met her,' he said. Ruby was so impressed; she gaped at the spectacle like a hungry fish.

Of course, she had seen many celebrities at the club. But this was different. Now she was a guest; she was one of them. Ruby nearly died when Garner introduced her to Barbara.

'We met the other night,' he said.

'Yes, we did and how lovely to meet you, my dear.'

'Oh, likewise,' said Ruby.

They tried to circulate but everyone was in little cliques and they couldn't break in. There was a sprinkling of celebrities there but most of them were the hangers-on who infest the world of glamour and who are ten times as snobbish and rude as the really famous.

Some people were dancing. Ruby wanted to join in but Garner said he didn't do things like that. For a start, he didn't like this kind of music. Not that he was any kind of aesthete, it just wasn't his bag. The raucous pop music was coming from a large record turntable in the corner, near the open French windows – just in case the neighbours couldn't hear it. The man who was changing the records was in the photograph at the charity do.

'Quick! Ruby! Who's that?' he said, grabbing her arm.

Ruby knew all the names. She read all the magazines and dreamed about the people in them. And now she was meeting them.

'He's a disc jockey on Radio Luxembourg. Oh, what's his name? …Jimmy Savile.'

Garner stored the name away. Savile didn't look very strong. He didn't look very charitable either. He had a huge cigar in his mouth and responded to requests by saying that he was paid to pick the music and could they go away. Garner didn't like a lot of people, but rarely had he been aware of such an instinctive repugnance. He decided for now that Savile was not someone he needed to pursue. That was one name taken off the suspects' list at least. They walked around and, as it was summer, strolled out into the garden. There were some more drunken dancers out there. Luckily, there was no pool for them to fall into.

'I thought Freddie was coming?' asked Ruby.

'He said he would. Maybe something came up.'

It would have been nice to see a friendly face. Before long, they ran into Diana again. She had come outside to make sure that no-one had started a bonfire with the garden chairs.

'Hello Scratch, hello Ruby.'

She remembered everyone's names. A born hostess.

'Having a good time?'

They said they were. Then, after a pause, Diana said to Garner, 'I'm glad you came tonight. There's a poker game starting upstairs in about half an hour. You might want to take a few hands.'

'Oh, he will!' said Ruby. 'He's briwyant at poker, aren't you, Wilson?'

'Call him Scratch, dear. The Prime Minister's called Wilson. We only want one of those. I'll tell the boys to expect you,' said Diana and bundled off again.

'I wish you hadn't said that,' said Garner.

'Oh, you don't have to play if you don't want to,' Ruby replied.

'I do now,' he said.

She was full of apologies.

'Don't worry,' he said. 'I've only got a few hundred with me. If I lose that, I'll call it quits.'

'Oh, but you won't lose, will you? Oh, Scratch, you don't want to lose hundreds of pounds.'

She wasn't sure whether she was horrified by the prospect or impressed with his insouciance.

'We'll see. Somehow, I don't feel lucky tonight.'

'Oh, Scratch, please don't play if you don't feel right,' she said. But she thought his comment was a bit odd since he had been telling her that poker was nothing to do with luck and was everything to do with skill. (This wasn't a lie for her sake: they all say this. It's complete garbage. You wouldn't think chess was a game of skill if someone dealt you all your pieces.)

'Don't play, Scratch. We can go now if you want. Nobody will mind and we've met all the famous faces.'

'It won't hurt to take a look,' he said.

After another drink and a few fruitless attempts to make friends, they both wandered upstairs.

CHAPTER TEN

Once above stairs, they went into the master bedroom which was being cleared for the game. The large bed had been pulled to one side and a table placed in the centre. Babs Windsor sat on the bed to watch her husband Ronnie Knight play. Sitting down, her pied mini-dress looked like a T-shirt. Sid James was there, although he was normally a horse player and a boxing man. He knew Mills well. He must have known Knight very well also, since he was making very free with his wife, putting his hand on her thigh and squeezing it every now and then. She would pretend to be outraged and then giggle.

James seemed quite approachable and was glad to talk to Ruby and Garner. They swapped tales of the track and of the ring, some of which might have been true. The other participants were unknowns. There was a man called Hokey who was short enough to be a jockey, although James didn't know him. There was also an Irish-looking woman with flame red hair who turned out to be American. Her name was Lillian. There was another couple of men – bland, undistinguished looking men - who gave their names so quietly that nobody heard them.

'Is this a friendly?' asked Scratch, as he sat down at the table.

'Friendly? There's no such thing,' said Lillian. She was right there. She looked at him as if he should have known that.

'House order of Diana,' said James, taking his chair. 'No bids higher than fifty quid. She doesn't want any knife fights in her recently decorated rooms.' He added his trademark cackle, 'Hyah, hyah hyah.'

'Understandable,' said Garner.

They sat around the table. No-one appointed Lillian the dealer, but it was assumed that she had been anointed to the role. She looked directly at Garner.

'You played in the States?' she asked.

'Sure, I've been around.'

'It's just that they tell me you're a hell of a gambler. I played all the big shots in New York, Chicago and Vegas. I never heard of you.'

Garner thought it might sound clever to say, 'I never heard of you either'. But it wasn't. Clearly, everyone in the US poker circuit knew her. Then he added, 'We ain't gonna make our reputations in this place tonight, so relax,' which was a bit better. Lillian shrugged and started dealing.

The first round was just a pacesetter in which everyone flexed his muscles and limbered up. The second round involved the loss of a few ten-shilling notes. Garner lost one of his. The third was a bit more lively with some fivers moving around. And so onwards and downwards. Garner realised, that real poker players weren't motivated by money but by the competition. They wanted to win if a bowl of rotten fruit had been the prize. James, by the way, got knocked out early by some reckless play. He tried to borrow some money from Barbara Windsor and then from Ronnie Knight and then from everyone in the room. His credit was bad. He sat with the spectators on the bed, making comments which only he found funny and then cackling at them. Not long after, Knight was out too, although he hadn't lost a lot.

The game went on. Before any of the players realised it, the watchers had drifted off. It was a long summer evening but soon, the lights were switched on. Only Ruby remained on the bed, looking increasingly horrified and bewildered as Garner took his drubbing.

He was down £50 – largely to Lillian who had not said a single word since she began dealing the cards. He suggested doubling the stakes as he had a good hand. He was holding three aces and was sure that nobody would beat it. Of course, he wasn't completely sure. He just didn't want to lose in front of Ruby.

Essentially, he was doing what he had done in the casino with Diana: namely, playing for show. He just assumed that the same genius of luck would be at his shoulder. Anyway, he could afford to lose a few hundred.

Now a minimum of £50 bet doesn't mean that you can only lose £50. It means that you can only bet £50 at a time. If someone throws in £100 and says 'double', then if your luck is out, you are £100 out. Scratch had had £300 in front of him on his pile and he had bet it all in £50 bits. Now he had to win or he was out of cash for the evening. Plus, he would look pretty stupid in front of Ruby. He called and turned over his three aces. The American lady had a flush.

Garner had lost but he wasn't going to take it lying down.

'Is my credit good?' asked Garner to the room. Ruby looked concerned.

'It's getting late, Scratch. You said you wanted to go soon.'

'Of course his credit is good,' said Diana from the doorway, where she had been silently watching for a while.

'He won £8,200 at the Grey Cat the other night, didn't you, Mississippi Johnny?'

She stood next to him and bounced him playfully with her hip.

'Oh, that's where I seen you,' said Lillian. 'You was in *Gone with the Wind*.'

There was some laughter, but the two silent men at the table hadn't come there to laugh.

'It was £15,000 he won,' said Ruby. Diana looked at her briefly, then ignored her.

'I thought you said no bets higher than £50?' said Garner.

'That was to protect the reckless Mr James from betting his house. If he still owns one. But I can make an exception for the Cincinnati Kid here.'

They played the next hand without limit. Garner had his cheque book on the table to back up a handful of markers. All the restraint he had shown at the Grey Cat was gone. And all his luck with it. The game went on and on relentlessly into the night. Either Garner found he had bad hands or he had good hands when someone else – usually Lillian – had better ones. By the time the game was over, he had lost £4000. His hand shook as he wrote the cheque.

'We must meet again,' said Lillian with an acid smile. 'I like the way you play.'

Freddie had been wise to stay away.

CHAPTER ELEVEN

After the game had broken up in silence, Garner went downstairs and asked to see Diana alone. As all the guests had left – apart from a few who couldn't – she took him into a small study.

'Bad night for you tonight, Scratch.'

'I'll survive.'

'I can't lend you any money if that's what this is about.'

'No, I'm OK. For now. Some you win, some you lose.'

'You shouldn't play with the big boys – or in this case, the big girls. You and I both know you won that money on the roulette table. What have you been telling that young girl?'

'That's my business.'

'Not in my house, sweetie, and not with her. I know her folks. I got her the job.'

Scratch reached into his pocket and pulled out the envelope. He took out the photo and showed it to her.

'That's you.'

'So? I'm in a lot of photographs.'

'Who are they?'

'Anyone could tell you that.'

'I know a few now - but not that character in the doorway. The one in the suit who looks handy.'

'Why?'

'Who won the competition?'

'What competition? It was a charity do.'

'So you do remember it.'

She handed him back the picture.

'Didn't they have a weightlifting competition?'

He made her look at it again.

'Heck, who knows? I was asked to lend my gracious and darling presence to promote a charity event for the kiddies' ward at a local hospital. I did what I was asked. I arrived, I kissed some people, I was photographed and I went home. I can't have been there more than fifteen minutes. I didn't have a drink and I paid for my own petrol. Are you happy now?'

'Who's the man in the shadow?'

'I don't know.'

'Take another look. Please. For me,' he added, as if 'for me' was like *Open Sesame*.

She took the picture again and looked at it hard, for a few minutes. Then, she said,

'She's a bit old to be a model.'

'Who?'

'Who? The model. The blonde model with the big cardboard cheque.'

'Never mind her. Who is he?'

She looked at him sharply, in a new way. There was no more wry amusement, just contempt.

'I can't help you Scratch,' she said forcing the picture back on him. 'Nobody can help you.'

'Who is it?'

'I'm doing you a favour by not telling you. Keep out of things like this. Burn that photo and go back to stealing hubcaps from ambulances. You're way out of your depth.'

'Who is it?'

'It's Freddie Foreman. He's the biggest gangster in South London. Now take your photo and your silly girlfriend and go home. And if you've got any money left, buy a new suit because that one's starting to look like it was glazed by Fanny Craddock.'

Garner ignored her.

'Why was he there? Freddie Foreman, I mean. What was he doing in a gym?'

'I don't know. Perhaps he likes skipping. Why the hell shouldn't he be in a gym? Is this interrogation over?'

Garner persevered.

'It doesn't make sense. Why would a top gangster be present at a charity function?'

Diana put her hands on her hips. She was getting ready for trouble and she was an intimidating sight. Her barbs were bouncing off Garner's stony carapace of indifference and she had had enough.

'I have no idea! Maybe he made all the bloody fairy cakes for the buffet. Why don't you go and ask him?'

She opened the door to the study and the audience was over.

Ruby had called a taxi. They rode in silence for most of the way home. Ruby said she was sorry a couple of times and Garner said, 'Forget it.' It wasn't really her fault. She had tried to get him to leave. She didn't know what to say, although she managed to resist the urge to say, 'Cheer up'.

But Garner was lost in his own woes. Now he needed that money. What money? Was there any money? Was there a crock of gold at the end of the trail? Garner had allowed himself to be dragged into an investigation without asking himself the most important question: namely, what was he going to do with the two lists once he found them? Perhaps he thought they would give him some negotiating power with the other people who had a claim on the proceeds. Perhaps he hadn't thought about it at all.

When they got back to the flat, the place had been turned over. They hadn't stripped off the wallpaper, so clearly the CIA wasn't responsible. But they'd had a good go at everything else. They'd even had the carpet up. Parts of it were stuck to the floor and had had to be cut. But Garner had the lists and the photo with him. They wouldn't have got anything.

Ruby was terrified.

'Oh, my goodness, you've been burgled!' she screamed. He grabbed her and told her to calm down.

'Ruby, there's nothing to worry about. There was no money here. They couldn't have taken anything of value. I've got my chequebook here... and the...'

'And what? What were they after Scratch? Were they looking for something?'

'It's better you don't know. Come on, I'll take you home.'

'No, I want to stay.'

She did her best to help him clear up the mess. By then the night was nearly over anyway. She had already stayed.

CHAPTER TWELVE

They were both still awake as it got light. They were lying together in bed. Garner looked at his watch. It was four-thirty.

'Wilson...Scratch,' she said. She lifted her head from his shoulder. 'You aren't in any trouble, are you?'

'Nothing I can't handle,' he said. She believed it, of course.

'I wouldn't want anything to happen to you. I like you so much.'

'I like you too.'

'I don't know what I'm going to tell me mother. I've never been out all night before.'

'What about the club?'

'That's different. They all know Freddie. Everyone likes Freddie. He wouldn't let anything happen to me. He takes me home or gets me a taxi. Like a father he is.'

'That's good. I wouldn't let anything happen to you either.'

'Oh, I know you wouldn't, Scratch. I know you wouldn't.'

She nestled close to him. She trusted him.

For a few days, they had a good time. The loss at cards was forgotten, since a man like Garner could only curse the bad luck which he had said was irrelevant in playing cards. He still had £4000 left and that went a long way in 1965. Scratch found a new place in a better area near Earls' Court. Located in a pleasant square, the flat was much grander. It boasted real, civilised amenities, including a washing machine. There was also a kitchen where you could cook stir-fry without knocking the window out with your elbow.

Being American, he would have been unaware that he was surrounded by Antipodeans. (Just as British people have trouble identifying Canadians.) He would have been aware, however, that the inhabitants of the locale were much louder and more confident than the diffident English. The area had more life to it. They behaved more like Americans, as if life were to be enjoyed rather than endured. He seemed to be going up in the world. The loss of half his fortune became sustainable.

They bought a few things together to decorate it. Ruby stayed a lot but was not the sort of girl to move in. He taught her how to make spaghetti, which, she said, her father would call 'foreign muck'. She made him roast beef and Yorkshire pudding. He was a pampered man.

They went to the cinema together. He wanted to see *Dr Terror's House of Horrors*. She wanted to see *The Sound of Music*. They compromised on *What's New Pussycat*? She laughed but thought it was very naughty. She didn't know much about most things, but her knowledge of film people was bottomless. She read all the magazines.

'That Peter Sellers is amazing. He can impersonate anyone.'

She nuzzled up to him in the dark theatre.

'He'd make a good conman.'

'Oh, Scratch! You shouldn't say things like that. I never know when you're being serious.'

He assured her that he was just kidding. She knew it all along. No conman would ever fool him, he explained. He read people too well.

They went to see *A Hard Day's Night* too. He told her that this proved how much he liked her.

'Oh, I can't believe you don't like the Beatles. They're fab.'

She couldn't make him believe that they wrote their own songs. And anyway, so what? Was he meant to be impressed? It was like saying they cut their own hair.

'They wouldn't want to come down to where I was brought up with haircuts like that.'

'Was that Chicago?'

'Yeah,' he said, but he could never be drawn further on the subject of his early life.

He bought her a television which allowed them to stay in more, something she was keen on, since going out to clubs was her work. He wasn't much interested himself. Programmes were just actors saying scripted words. None of it was real, he said. British TV was unbelievably dull anyway.

He couldn't believe her when she asked if he had a licence.

'A licence? What for?'

'For the television. You have to have a licence to watch television in this country.'

'You're kidding me? A licence to watch TV? What is this, Russia? A licence to drive I can understand that.'

He could understand it, although of course he did not have one. Not a legitimate one, anyway. But he knew he was a good driver, so it didn't matter. They got a TV licence at her insistence. She even paid for it herself out of her own money.

They watched as the extraordinary decade flooded into their little space. President Johnson began sending more and more boys to get slaughtered in order to salvage his stubborn pride over Vietnam.

'Did you vote for him?' she asked as they sat on the sofa watching the news.

'Me? I don't vote.'

'Oh, but you should. You should vote, Scratch.'

'Bunch of phonies. Look at that bastard Johnson sending all those fools to die in the middle of nowhere.'

'I'm sure they all do their best. The politicians, I mean. Do you think we'll win?'

'We? Who's we? Anyway, there's no-one to fight. Just a bunch of phantoms. You think I'd go? Not me. The world's going crazy,' he said, switching off the television. American cities were burning in riots. News from America had started to depress him. But there was no escape from the world. One day at the cinema, they watched a Pathe News report about Ed White, the American astronaut doing the first spacewalk.

'Gosh, that's amazing,' said Ruby. 'Fancy walking out in space. I'd never be brave enough to do that. You must be very proud. You know, being American and all that.'

Garner spread his hands out in mystification. She took this to mean that he was speechless with wonder. But Garner didn't want to see reality on the screen. He wanted to avoid the world. Didn't people go to the movies for escape? But the news was everywhere around them.

After they had watched the film, they went back to his apartment and went to bed.

Garner rarely dreamed. His nights were usually as black as his days. And, as his waking hours were most often spent in the darkness of the late evenings and early mornings of clubs and dives, it meant that he saw very little in the way of illumination in any part of his life.

But this night he dreamed. He dreamed that he was on a spacewalk. And the lifeline which connected him to the capsule had broken. He was drifting away into space, on and on. Not towards the sun but into the eternal black of the cosmos. There were no stars in Garner's universe, just the lightless and timeless void. And he drifted on and on into it without end. It was not a nightmare and he did not wake up screaming or covered in perspiration. He just awoke with a strange feeling of inertia. Had he been better educated, he might have called it a philosophical inertia. But a better educated man wouldn't have felt like that. A man of education wouldn't have been in his state.

Ruby had already gone. He wondered what excuse she gave to her parents. Working at the club, or something? Would her parents believe that the club opened almost every night? She just came and went. He was glad when she came but also glad when she left. He could not imagine how people – like her parents – could get married and stay in each other's company for the rest of their lives.

He watched in equal bewilderment as she enjoyed her pop music programmes: *Ready Steady Go* and *Thank Your Lucky Stars*. Guys with hair like girls. He complained about the very things that made Ruby attractive. Raging against the indecency of mini-skirts, while allowing his girlfriend to strut about in a nightclub in fishnets and a basque. He was not a man of sophistication. He did not realise that there was a time when women showing their ankles was considered an outrage. He was not unique amongst people in thinking that the age he had been born into was normal, everything before it was dull and restrictive, while everything coming in to disturb the equilibrium was the Apocalypse. It was the Apocalypse all right, but it was a slow-burn Apocalypse that had started a long time before Garner began thinking about it.

Times change, but the changes came ever faster and nothing seemed to stem the tide. Wave after wave of new sensations and fashions hurled themselves relentlessly against the sense of security and stability which humans need to stay sane. Every day brought new outrages and more bad news. He wanted to stop it but was utterly powerless. He started to fear what the television showed him. He feared the future but he was not capable of fearing *for* the future. It is not long before people who fear the future start to fear the present. And he began to want what all such people wanted: the wherewithal to build himself a refuge from it all. This created a new hunger in him which went beyond comfort and survival. It was a hunger that began focusing itself on the pursuit of the list. He began to believe it was the key to everything.

And yet, for all his anxieties over what was to come, he still held a curious and misplaced faith in his own destiny. Naturally, he had never given a second's thought to the meaning of life or the course of history. But if the world was tumbling into madness in the long term, he took it for granted that nothing could interfere with his own pursuit of life, love, liberty, happiness and self-fulfilment.

Garner knew instinctively – for he was a man of total instinct – that despite the pitfalls and frustrations which the immediate world offered; despite the horrors of the future – whether Doomsday or dementia - all would be well with himself. The afflictions of existence, he knew, were only for others. Thus, he could see himself heading towards victory while the world around him collapsed. In this, he was something of a child, seeing the passage of time as a leisurely flow into the gentle infinite, with all accounting held at bay, rather than a desperate cascade across the rapids towards inevitable oblivion.

CHAPTER THIRTEEN

One night Ruby took Scratch to meet her parents in their small, terraced house on the Strone Road. Strone was a legendary long road of terraced houses that ran through East London. It wasn't one of those areas where the primary use of a pram is to fetch scavenged coal, but it was not middle class either. Each house was much like the one next door.

Inside, there was an old piano in the hall, which, in accordance with tradition, had never been tuned. At the front was a parlour, which was only used if the vicar dropped in, Ruby said. At the end of the hall was a slim dining room and beyond that, an even smaller kitchen. The house was probably quite adequate for the family's needs, as long as there were three bedrooms upstairs. If you looked out of the front windows upstairs, you could see the trolley bus wires.

Her parents welcomed him politely. Her father, Donald, had worked on the railways for thirty years as an engineer. It was a dirty job, but he polished his shoes every morning before he went to work. He was one of those traditional men, rugged and bald, who was brave in the face of danger but uncertain and nervous in the face of authority. He was only fifty but looked as though retirement was close.

Her mother Madge was a housewife, who produced sandwiches, cakes and tea. The day was divided into two for Madge. For one half, she wore curlers in her chestnut hair and for the other half, she didn't. The first half was preparation for the second.

Donald suggested they eat in the parlour. Garner hoped that the vicar wouldn't be coming. He had not really wanted to go but Ruby had insisted. It was agreed, however, before they went that Garner would claim a more respectable profession. They decided upon the vending industry, since Garner had at least some knowledge of fruit machines. She was rapidly becoming his willing accomplice in constructing fantasies.

Her parents liked him. This was more bad luck than bad judgment on their part or winning charm on his part. At first, they may have been worried that he was much older than she was; but this worked to Garner's advantage. He compared very favourably with her brother Tommy, who was proving somewhat troublesome at the moment. And, as most of the trouble stemmed from his exposure to youth culture involving pop music, parties and long hair, it was not surprising that they breathed a sigh of relief at the sight of Garner in his suit and Navy haircut. Tommy joined them reluctantly. His father told him to comb his hair first.

'State of his barnet!' he said, apologetically, to Garner. 'Look at him!' He didn't know what got into kids these days. It was television. It was the Beatles. It was the newspapers. He and Garner agreed to share the blame around on the usual suspects. In this matter, they were almost on the same side.

The second reason Donald liked Garner was that he was a jazz fan and Garner liked jazz. Actually, he didn't. Garner had almost no interest in music of any kind, although he knew he loathed modern music. But he knew about jazz as he had grown up with it. He knew the difference between Chicago Jazz and traditional jazz. He knew who Charlie Parker and Benny Goodman were. Donald told him about all the English jazz players like Acker Bilk, and Garner pleased Ruby by feigning interest and listening politely. Thus, when Garner talked of the clubs he knew 'back home', Donald naturally associated them with music rather than gambling or drinking dens or other activities which prospered in the furtive atmosphere of dark places under the sidewalk.

'Did I ever tell you about when I met Buddy Rich?' said Garner to them.
'You've met Buddy Rich?' said Donald in wonder.
'Sure I have.'
And Garner, quick on his feet, outlined a story about his meeting with the notoriously obnoxious drummer. (He hadn't tried anything with Garner, you may be sure of that!) It may have been true, it may have been false. It didn't matter with a man like Garner. Why would it matter if it *was* true or false? The past was a phantom. It didn't exist anywhere. It could be anything.

And of course, he knew Freddie Mills. They knew and liked Freddie. But that also brought sport into the equation which was a big plus with Donald. Also, the fact was true – Ruby could attest to it - and it made the untrue stories more believable. Any friend of Freddie was a friend of theirs. Did Garner like boxing? Sure, he loved boxing. He was home and dry. Her father liked a good fight. Her mother liked him because her father did. And because he knew celebrities like Diana Dors. A man who knew people in films must have been a safe bet. They wouldn't mix with bad people: it would be bad for their careers. Ruby had told them that Garner had taken them to Diana's house. The way she told it, you'd think they'd been there for a musical soiree. So, all was well. Telling untruths was becoming easier and easier for her by the day.

Nonetheless, Garner felt uncomfortable with them. But strangely, he got on well with the brother Tommy. Tommy was seventeen and was playing in a pop combo. He was somewhat vague about which instruments he played; and he had trouble remembering which gigs they had performed at recently. (It was a vagueness that Garner recognised from some of his own reminiscences.) But he did have an acoustic guitar in his bedroom and his mother was convinced that he was talented. He just needed to settle down. Tommy wanted to hear the stories about Chicago and Garner was glad to fabricate one. Madge told him not to pester Mr Garner and let him drink his tea. But Garner insisted he was only too happy to tell him some Chicago stories. They would have a talk sometime. Just him and Tommy. Definitely. Tommy thought Garner was glamorous and dangerous and began to look up to him.

And Garner made sure, at Ruby's prompting, to tell Madge how much he had enjoyed the cakes.

CHAPTER FOURTEEN

The club was starting to look normal to Garner when it was empty. He arrived at about 11.30am one morning. Two men were just coming out of the office. They didn't look like autograph hunters. They weren't the two men who had killed Dessau, but they had probably gone to the same finishing school.

'You've got three days, Freddie,' said one of them.

Then they left. Garner walked into the office. Mills was sitting behind the desk which didn't look any tidier than it had the last time he was there. The pile of final demands might have been a bit higher. There was no sign of Mr Ho. Mills looked distracted as he said,

'Scratch. Nice to see you again.'

He motioned to the other chair and Garner sat.

'Trouble?'

'Nothing I can't handle. What can I do for you?'

'Didn't see you at the party at Diana's.'

'No, I was erm...something came up.'

'I got into a card game.'

'Yes, I heard a whisper. Lose much?'

'Four grand.'

Mills closed his eyes and sucked in some breath.

'Painful,' he said.

'Well, easy come, easy go.'

'Well, easy go, anyway.'

They both tried for a laugh but weren't really in the mood. Garner reached into his pocket and took out the newspaper clipping.

'You send me this?'

'What is it?'

'Take a look. Do you recognise it?'

'Send it to you? No, why would I?'

He said it fast, without properly looking at it.

'Take a better look.'

'Well, of course I remember it. I was there, obviously. I remember the occasion. But no, why would I send it to you?'

Garner turned the cutting over.

'But that is your writing on the back?'

'Sure, but I didn't send it. Why would I? How would I know your address?'

'They took it at the door when I registered.'

'All right, we've got your address. But I didn't send it.'

'You being careful with the stamps, huh? If you didn't send it. then who did?'

'You got me, mate. Here, have a drink.'

Mills got up and opened a small cupboard in the corner of the room. He took out a small bottle and poured a scotch for Garner but didn't take one himself. Then he sat down again. Garner didn't think he had seen him drink properly.

'Let's get everything out in the light where we can see it, Freddie. You got money problems. I don't, but I just took a hit. I can't afford to retire yet. Now this list and the Chinese box that goes with it might be the answer to our difficulties.'

'Which difficulties are these? And what items are these and why would they help us?'

'Oh, come on. Those two guys I just saw, they weren't here to read the gas meter.'

'Look, Scratch, that's just a cutting from a local rag.'

Garner leaned forward.

'Who was the strongest?'

'You what?'

'Who was the strongest? Who lifted that barbell?'

'Gordon Bennett, man! I don't know. We were just messing about for charity. Comedy capers in a gym with sporting celebrities. Those two wrestlers, Pallo and McManus, right? Their public thinks they're rivals, enemies. They're great mates. They work on routines together. It's all a joke. You know what wrestling is. It's all rigged.'

'Sometimes boxing is too.'

'Yeah, don't I know it? But I never threw a fight. I was asked to, but I never did.'

'Never said you did. I saw one of your fights at the movies. You were good. You never give up. That's a quality I like in anyone. I'm a little that way myself.'

'Yeah well, that was a long time ago. Let's not relive past glories, eh?'

'Why not? You should celebrate them. I never had any myself.'

They both laughed, properly this time.

'Look,' said Garner, 'somebody sent me that clipping. Somebody who knew I was with Lucky Len the night he died. The guys who came after him were after a list and a Chinese box. See, I'm being straight with you.'

'Yeah, you're being dead candid, mate. Where's the list?'

'How would I know?'

'Do me a favour. You came here asking about a Chinese box.'

'Like the one Mr Ho had.'

'Similar but different. But you never asked for any list. You wouldn't want the box without the list. Now where is it?'

'That's my business. And what you just said, shows you know about this.'

Mills leaned forward, showing some aggression for the first time.

'I've had conversations like this before. You want me to tell you everything but you don't want to tell me anything.'

'I've admitted I've got the list. Where's the box? Somewhere there is another box with the second list in.'

'So you say. What is this second list?'

'Don't you know? They're no good without each other. The first is useless without the second.'

'You've been reading too many comics, mate.'

'Yeah, I read 'em at the barber's. I get my haircut regular. I must be the only person in this crazy country under fifty who does. Why was Freddie Foreman there?'

'He lives local. The gym's in Streatham. It's not a corrupt place, especially, but he goes there. It's one of those places. He probably knows a lot of people who go there for work outs. The Five Star, it's called. Don't ask me why. Egon Ronay wouldn't give it one star. Neither would Genghis Khan.'

Both men leaned back. They laughed again. Mills got up and went to the cupboard as if to offer Scratch another drink. Or maybe have one himself. But when he opened it, the bottles were empty. He sat down again.

'Freddie, I'm trying to help you.'

'Thanks for your concern, Scratch. I'll sort my own problems out.'

'Really? The other day, you wanted a loan from me.'

'I'm always keen to help new investors break into the market.'

'So, you're not gonna help me?'

'I don't know what you want. It all seems a bit dangerous to me. Dangerous or crazy. Maybe both.'

'Yeah, my apartment was turned over.'

'Oh, for crying out loud man, you don't think I did that, do you? I'm not Al Capone. I don't do things like that.'

'No, I guess not. I never really figured it was you.'

'Listen, if this list – these lists – really exist, then someone wants them. Someone a lot nastier than me.'

He leaned forward again, but with less aggression. He rested his arms on the desk.

'Now look, Scratch, we both like each other. I'd estimate you've got four grand left. That's still a lot of money. Now I realise you can't retire on it but you're not in any hurry. Have a think about the next step. Carefully.'

'What do you want me to do? Go to night school?'

'You could do dumber things.'

'Yeah, I could become a boxer.'

'No, you couldn't Scratch. You'd need certain qualities that you don't have.'

Garner ignored this. He had questions to ask.

'Why did you write 'To the strongest the spoils' on the back?'

'I don't know. Just a joke. Don't get all involved in things.'

Mills got up to signal that he wanted Garner to go.

'Are we good?' he asked.

'Sure.'

Garner stood up. They shook hands. There was a short silence as both men tried and failed to weigh each other up.

'Now, just before you go, what about the investment? This club is on the up. My problems are temporary. I need a bridging loan and the terms could be generous.'

'You mean I'm the last one to get beaten up by those guys?'

He threw his head back to the door to indicate the men who had left. Mills said nothing to this.

'The Five Star Gym in Streatham?'

'Oh, now don't go poking around down there, Scratch. They won't know anything.'

'How do you know they won't know anything?'

'Because there isn't anything to know. Not in that photo anyway.'

'That's my concern.'

'Well, it's your life, your time and your money. If I was you...'

'Yeah, I know. If you were me, you'd go into the nightclub business, maybe.'

'Don't be too long making the decision.'

'You under pressure? I mean a lot?'

'Like I say, nothing I can't handle.'

There was no problem anywhere that people couldn't handle. Garner put his hand on the door and then asked one more question.

'Those two – they practise at the Five Star?'

'Yeah, sure. Not today. Tomorrow. And not until the afternoon – usually about three. They won't want any interruptions. But you won't listen to advice to be cautious, will you?'

Garner shrugged and left. He went round the back of the club and sat in his car for a while. Mills was right, he thought. Pallo and McManus probably wouldn't know anything. But he had to talk to everyone in the picture. Mills and Dors were holding out on him. People had been told to be quiet. Any clue might be vital. Something was going on around him and he felt like a fool in the middle of a merry-go-round.

That night, Ruby and Garner took Tommy out for a drink. He wasn't technically old enough to buy alcoholic drinks in a pub but seventeen could pass for eighteen.

Garner got a good look at the lad for the first time. He was neither handsome nor ugly. His unruly mop of brown hair was dull and stringy. It was starting to reach his collar but was already receding at the temples. In ten years' time he would be as bald as his father. If he was in a group, he couldn't be the singer, even if he could sing. Truthfully, there was not much that was remarkable about him. He could go bad, he could go good. Just a little nudging in one direction or another would decide the course of his life.

'You go to the same barber as the Beatles?' Garner had kidded him.

'I don't go to the barber,' said Tommy and they all laughed. Then Garner sent Tommy to the bar to get the drinks. When he came back with them, he offered Garner his change but Garner said, 'Keep it.'

'Blimey, thanks Mr Garner.'

'Scratch. Call me Scratch. Don't stand on ceremony. We ain't at Buckingham Palace.'

Garner offered him a cigarette. Tommy looked uncertainly at Ruby. If he already smoked, clearly she didn't know. Garner caught the look.

'Come on... Your sister sells them for a living, Tommy.'

Tommy smiled, shrugged and took one. You could tell by the way he lit it that he had smoked before.

'You'll get me shot,' said Ruby. But she smoked as well.

'I bet you've met some characters back in Chicago, Scratch.'

'Well, sure. I won't kid you I knew Al Capone. He was a little before my time.'

He wondered if he should say his father had met him. But he had already told them he never knew his father. It must have irritated him to have cornered himself by telling the truth about something. However, he did tell some stories: about the people he had known and the things they got up to. Whatever scrapes he had been in he had gotten out of by his own cleverness and daring. Ruby was as rapt as Tommy.

'Sure,' said Garner, winding up his litany of tales. 'I started out by doing a few bad things. Doesn't mean you're a bad person.'

'Oh, careful Scratch,' said Ruby. 'Don't give him ideas.'

'Nobody's giving him ideas,' said Garner. 'He's a clever kid. Knows what he wants. He'll go his own way.'

Tommy asked him if he knew the Great Train Robbers. Garner told him not to ask. He wasn't to talk about that. It was his most impressive story. If Tommy hadn't been sold then, he was now.

CHAPTER FIFTEEN

Garner was determined to go forwards. But there was no point in doing anything until he had a new car. It was obviously his car that had allowed them to track him down.

There were plenty of car dealers in London, some of them honest. But he didn't want to go to one recommended by anyone. If someone advised it, then someone knew about it; and that meant they could trace him. But he also needed one who wasn't totally legitimate. He didn't want anyone looking too closely at his documentation.

The next day he found a suitable forecourt in Lewisham, in Southeast London. It was part second-hand car showroom and part junk yard. Looking at the stock on show, it wasn't easy to tell the difference.

The man in charge had more of the junkyard in him than the car salesman. He was polishing the windscreen of an old Anglia with a cloth like sandpaper. He might have been trying to remove fingerprints. Garner parked up and went over to him. The man nodded as if there was nothing in the world he hated more than customers.

'Hi. I want to get rid of my car.'

'Oh yeah?' said the man. 'Moving up to Formula 1, are you?'

He said it with suspicion because law-abiding people usually say they want to buy a new one rather than dispose of an old one. Not that it mattered: the man was obviously a crook, although Garner didn't think it was the right place to buy a getaway car.

'Sure,' said Garner. 'I've been here before. I buy all my Swiss watches from you.'

After a bit of half-hearted haggling, he traded in his car for a Ford Cortina. (He'd wanted a Pontiac but it probably wouldn't have fitted on the roads.) It wasn't a flashy model, but he had new priorities now. The car wasn't meant to impress debutantes and film directors but to get him around in his search. The trade-in cost him £200. Bit by bit, his expenses were mounting. In only a few days, he had halved his fortune. There must have been a line at which he could not go any further. A line at which any gambler cuts his losses and goes home. But the crock of gold was there, beckoning him on.

There was a little portacabin office in which the car salesman, who clearly also doubled as a breaker's yard operative, filled out the necessary forms. (Some of the forms were deemed not necessary and had been omitted from the transaction, even though they were legal requirements.) The man didn't look comfortable wielding a pen. While he was tidying up the admin behind a desk with no chairs to sit on, Garner noticed that there was a local paper in the in-tray.

'You advertise in this?'

'Yeah.'

'Local paper?'

'Well, it ain't the bleedin' Financial Times now, is it?' said the man. He continued writing with his tongue between his teeth, breathing heavily. He was obviously a man of the outdoors. Admin bored him, if he was honest. Truth be told, he was only really happy when he was burning tyres.

Garner leaned on the wall and looked at the paper. It was a cheaply produced local rag, mainly full of classified ads but with a few paltry news items. The stories were concerned with things like whether the local council said Yes or No to a new supermarket near the ring road. Stuff like that. There was an address on the back.

'Is Peckham far from here?'

'No. Same time zone.'

He gave Scratch the documents and concluded with a short lecture about how if anything went wrong with the car, he was not to come and bother them because his rights were basically nil.

'Oh, before you go, if you're interested, I can actually get hold of Swiss watches too.'

'Yeah, I'll bet. I prefer the ones that come from Switzerland.'

'That's the problem with you Yanks: you're too choosy.'

'Why else would I come to your place?'

'Is anyone likely to come looking for your old car?'

'Yeah, the Queen Mother made me an offer.'

'We do a special crushing service if you're interested.'

'For the car or the Queen Mother?'

None of this banter was said with amusement or friendliness. It was pure cold ritual.

Scratch had plenty of time until three 'o' clock, so he decided to pay the paper a visit.

When he got to Peckham, he found a small building in a backstreet – of course. The property had obviously once been a house and was now split up into three offices. There was a sign saying *Reception* over one of those sliding frosted windows. The door would be locked: newspapers attract nutters. There was a bell which Garner pressed. He didn't hear anything, so he pressed it again. Then he knocked on the window. After a few minutes, it was opened by a small, grubby, squinting little man with grubby fingers. He was wearing a brown work overall. He had brown hair and brown fingers to match. Whatever the hell Mary Quant was up to that year, as far as this man was concerned, brown was the season's must-have colour. He was eating a sandwich. That was brown as well. The daylight seemed to bother him. It might have been his first time above ground.

'Hi, my name's Templeton,' said Garner.

The man had no interest at all in this piece of information. Garner showed him the photograph.

'Did your paper print this?'

'I don't know.'

'Yeah, what I mean is, how can I find out?'

'I dunno.'

'Is there someone else I can talk to?'

'No.'

Garner took out his wallet and offered the man a pound note.

'What's that?'

'It's a pound note.'

'What's that for?'

'Just an incentive to help you help me.'

'I don't want it. There's no-one here.'

'Well, is there a manager there I can talk to?' said Garner, trying to control his anger.

'No.'

'There must be someone else. Where's the staff?'

'Lunchtime.'

Garner wanted to hit him.

'When will they be back?' he shouted.

'Two 'o' clock,' said the man, closing the window.

Garner went to find a fish and chip shop and got some dinner. He sat in his new car and ate it. The car stank afterwards. When it was after two, he went back to the little newspaper. He knocked on the frosted window. This time a middle-aged woman who looked like an antiquarian bookshop assistant opened the window. She was wearing a twinset cardigan and top and had glasses on a chain around her neck. She would have called them spectacles, without a doubt. He couldn't see what else she was wearing but it had to be a tweed skirt. Garner thought this was an encouraging sign.

'Yes?' she said.

'Hello, there. My name is Templeton. I'm a private detective.'

'A private detective? What's a private detective?' she said, as if she hadn't quite heard him.

Garner managed to prevent himself from saying, 'You're kidding me, right?'

'Did the other guy tell you I'd called?'

'No. What other man?'

He was only confusing the issue so he took out the increasingly tired-looking photograph.

'Could you tell me if your newspaper printed this?'

The woman put on her spectacles and looked at the picture.

'I don't remember it. When was it?'

'A few months ago. Is there a photographer who might remember it?'

She shook her head.

'This is a local trading paper. We mainly take advertising from local companies and tradesmen. Any news items are normally sent to us, or written by people who want to pretend that they're news items when they're really adverts. The photographers would be freelance. They would sell the photos to us. Or they would come from a stringer. An agency. Something like that. We don't actually gather news here.'

'Would I be able to find out who took it?'

'Well, that would depend on how important a matter it was. You would have to talk to a lot of people, I should imagine. If it's important, it should be a job for the police.'

'No, it's not like that. Nobody's in trouble. It was just a charity event for a local hospital. With celebrities and stuff. Wouldn't you remember that?'

'No. They normally take their own photos. It doesn't look like a professional job. But I'm not an expert. We don't even do the printing here. It's just an office. Just myself and a telesales girl. And Bob. He's the caretaker.'

'Was that Bob I spoke to?'

'Possibly.'

'Tell him he should go into politics.'

There was a pause. The woman stared at him as if she were waiting for something. Then Garner remembered he was in England.

'Thanks very much. You've been most helpful.'

The woman gave him one of his own tight smiles back and said,

'You're very welcome. I'm sorry I couldn't be of more assistance.'

She closed the window and Garner walked away. He went back to his car and had a cigarette.

Across the road was a huge line of people waiting for a bus that wasn't going to come. They were standing in front of a billboard saying, *It's better by bus!* He sympathised with the frustrated commuters. He was really getting nowhere now, just like them.

Now he came to think about it, he wasn't even sure if the photographer would have been able to tell him anything useful. It had been a long shot. And it hadn't paid off. Of course it hadn't. They never do.

It was half past two. He was ready to go to the Five Star Gym. He drove to Streatham, found the place on the High Street and parked up.

Inside, there was not much of the five star about the place, as Freddie had said. It was a gym like any other. A few pugs were thumping punch balls and punchbags. There didn't seem to be any amazing pugilistic talent there. They were just keeping their circulation going. In the middle of the place was a ring for either boxing or wrestling, or possibly keeping the pigs in.

Two men were in the ring. They saw Garner and gave him a hearty South London welcome.

'Oo the 'ell are you?'

'Name's Wilson Garner. People call me Scratch. I think you're Jackie Pallo. Seen you on TV. I'd like a word, if that's OK.'

Pallo was a smallish, stocky man who wore a trademark little pigtail, like an eighteenth-century Italian opera director. He climbed out of the ring and grabbed a towel to wipe the perspiration from himself. The towel had been to the same laundry that served his local café. The other man, McManus, leaned on the ropes and watched him from the ring.

'Either one of you will do. I'd like to show you a picture.'

'Oh,' said McManus, 'careful Jack, he wants to show you his etchings.'

'I'll have you know I'm engaged,' said Pallo.

They both laughed.

'Great stuff,' said Garner flatly. 'I hear Bob Hope's looking for writers again.'

'I should think he bloody well is. He needs them.'

'What I want won't take a second and then you can carry on with your dance routine.'

He pulled out the envelope, removed the clipping and showed them the picture.

'What's this?' asked Pallo.

'I believe that's you,' said Garner. 'And that's your friend.'

'Two more handsome characters I never saw,' said Pallo.

'We don't do autographs,' said McManus. And they both chuckled again.

'So what if it is us?' said Pallo.

'Yeah, so what?' said his brother-in-arms.

'I'd like to ask you some questions about it.'

'Why? What for? Who the hell are you?' said Pallo. But Garner rather got the impression that they already knew.

'I'm researching for a BBC drama,' said Garner, which rejoinder may or may not have been funny but was certainly not helpful. This was not going as planned, he thought. Except of course that he hadn't made any plan. Pallo folded his arms.

'What exactly do you want to know?'

'Who was the strongest?'

'What?'

Pallo turned to his friend who returned his quizzical expression. Amazing how much surprise and confusion that question evoked.

'Who was the strongest?'

'He's a nutter,' said McManus. 'Throw him out.'

'That was taken months ago. I've been to sleep since then. In front of the telly. Usually Coronation Street. Gets me off just like that.'

'Yeah, sure, I know. It was some kind of competition. All the celebrities tried to lift the barbell or something. Who won?'

The answer from the two men was routine. It hadn't really been a competition, it was a charity do. A bit of a laugh. Freddie Mills was a famous comic character. Money raised for the local hospital for kids. There was no competition.

'Who lifted the barbell?'

McManus came down out of the ring.

'Nobody,' he said. 'That weighs over 360lbs. No man could have lifted that.'

'Sorry Mr Garner. Can't help you.'

'Nobody wants to talk about it,' said Garner.

'Maybe nobody wants to talk to *you*,' said Pallo, smiling and putting his arm around Garner.

'Yeah, you should try some of that new after shave they're advertising on the telly,' put in his friend.

'Gentlemen, I've come a long way and I only had one question: Who was the strongest?

'We'll show you,' said McManus. And they started to grab hold of him.

Garner liked to think he could have handled one of them easily enough. After all, he was a big guy and while they were trained wrestlers, a lot of what they did was for entertainment.

They didn't hit him or rough him up at all. They just grabbed him, one end each and put him out on the street. They thought it was a very amusing routine. He struggled, but it wasn't violent enough to warrant an escalation. And he didn't want the police being called.

Garner felt foolish, but there was no-one around to laugh at him. He walked back to his new car and sat at the steering wheel for a while. He could still smell the fish and chips. It was a warm day and he opened the window.

Clearly, someone had put out the word that he was not to be helped. One stupid question was all he had to ask. The photo was becoming worthless now. He knew almost everyone in it. He debated for a while going to see Freddie Foreman. Did you go and see a man like Freddie Foreman? How would you find him? It might be easier than you would think. Criminals these days didn't seem to live in the shadows. They stood in the light and posed for the cameras. They went to charity events. They'd be advertising Fairy Snow washing powder soon. Maybe he was in the Classified Ads under 'Villain'. You've tried the rest, now try the best. With customer testimonials from the Archbishop of Canterbury, the well-known television personality.

He started the new car and drove very slowly back home, stopping at all the lights.

CHAPTER SIXTEEN

What the men did, they did really well. It was perfectly planned and executed. There was intelligence behind it.

Garner had only just parked the car and was getting out, when a man appeared from nowhere and blocked him. He heaved against the man, which action distracted him while the second man got in the back seat and held a knife to his throat. He stopped pushing against the door. The first man then walked calmly round and got into the passenger seat. Then he took out a gun.

'Drive,' said the man in the front. Garner started up the car and pulled out.

'Where?'

'It doesn't matter,' said the man in front. 'It's a lovely day. Haven't you heard? Half the joy of travelling is in the journey. It must be true: somebody on television said it.'

'We'll direct you,' said the man with the knife.

He recognised them all right. The one behind was the boxer and the man in front was the one with the trilby, although he wasn't wearing it at the moment. Was he going to get the same treatment as Dessau? True, that had not been an intended outcome. They hadn't meant to kill Dessau, but now that they *had* killed him, they knew that Garner had been a witness.

'It's a warm day,' said the boxer. 'You're going for a swim.'

The man in front waited just long enough for this to frighten Garner before saying,

'Maybe. It all depends.'

Garner looked in the rear-view mirror at the boxer. (He didn't dare look to the side.) He had been punched in the face by everyone in the world except Mahatma Gandhi. One of his ears looked like a small omelette. *Who would have hired him as an enforcer?* thought Garner. But he had to admit they were doing well so far. They had the upper hand.

Garner drove himself and the men, obeying their instructions, until they came to the river. They were at a sort of wharf. He didn't know where he was.

They made him park the car at the top of a concrete boat runway down to the water. Garner took rather thin comfort from the fact that there were witnesses there. The man with the gun ordered him to get out. Then he hid the gun in his jacket pocket.

Once they were all out, the boxer opened the doors and windows of the car and then took off the handbrake. Then he pushed the car down the runway.

'Wheeee!' he said.

All the people stopped and stared as the car plunged down into the river. The man with the trilby, who wasn't wearing his trilby, turned to the crowd and said,

'It's an advert.'

Both the men thought this was most amusing. So did one or two of the bystanders. Garner was meeting a lot of humourists today.

They all watched as the car bubbled and gurgled downwards.

'Next time,' said the boxer, pointing to the new car as it sank out of sight, 'you're inside it.'

'And the doors won't be open,' said the man with the gun.

With impressive precision, another car drew up and the two men got in and disappeared.

Garner had only just bought that car. Now he had to buy another. He moved off quickly before someone called the police. He began to realise how expensive taxis were in England.

CHAPTER SEVENTEEN

Garner got home and flopped on the bed. He was bone tired and going round in circles. He knew he would have to buy a new car. He couldn't claim on the insurance: too many questions would be asked. Plus, he didn't have any. That could all wait until tomorrow, he hoped. He slept for a while and was awoken by the phone. At first, he wasn't sure if he wanted to answer it. But not knowing was worse than knowing. And if it was trouble, they couldn't do much over the telephone line, except warn him that trouble was coming, which he knew anyway. It was Ruby, calling from a phone box. And it was trouble. The line bleeped as she put her money in.

'Scratch... it's me.'

Again, he took the number and called her back.

'Are you OK?'

She wasn't OK. She was crying.

'I'm pregnant.'

Of course, he asked her if she was sure. That was the stock response.

'Yes, of course I'm sure. My Dad will kill me.'

'OK, just relax. Everything will be all right. Get a cab. Come over here. I'll pay for it.'

'All right. I'm coming.'

She said something else, but he wasn't listening. He put down the phone slowly. The shadows were starting to lengthen. And he was no longer feeling lucky. Then he had a caller.

The knock on the door was the practised knock of someone who knocked for a living. Either he was selling something, or he was a Jehovah's Witness or it was the police. He opened the door to see a stocky, greying man in his fifties. He was wearing a suit which he wore to work everyday. The visitor was obviously a policeman. People from Garner's background knew them instinctively. But they normally came in pairs as mutual witnesses - unless they were up to something.

'Mr Garner?'

'Yuh.'

'My name is Williams. Detective Inspector Frank Williams of the Flying Squad. May I come in?'

The Flying Squad. They dealt with big gangs and violent crime. They had famously chased, caught and jailed the Great Train Robbers. Well, most of them. Williams had been a leading light in that investigation.

'What do you want?'

'There's no trouble. This visit is quite unofficial. I just wanted a small chat, really.'

Garner opened the door wide and waved the policeman in. It would have been unwise to do anything which suggested that he had anything to hide. And to be perfectly fair, Garner was not always unwise. In the light he could see that Williams was probably near retirement – a state which always seems to be nearer for the police than it does for other workers. He spoke with a noticeable accent, although Garner would not have known that it was Welsh.

Williams looked tired. Garner had seen the look before. It was a common look for policemen wherever you met them. A kind of occupational exhaustion caused by the huge expenditure of energy for so little return. Two or maybe three-year investigations which fall apart because a witness changes his mind suddenly. Or because some slimy lawyer puts a known killer back on the street on a technicality. It came from fighting against a rising tide of crime and a thickening mass of legal brambles which hindered the authorities and assisted the criminals. Of course, Garner knew that there were prosecutors as well as defendants. But he hated all lawyers, much more than he hated the cops. He had that much in common with humanity, at least. Not that he was sympathetic. He wasn't in the least sympathetic. But he knew the police. He had met so many and listened to their tales of woe. No wonder they retire so early, he thought.

'Thank you. As I say, this isn't exactly an official visit. I just wanted to go over a few things. May I sit?'

'Help yourself. I like listening to stories.'

Williams sat on the only armchair and looked around at the flat. Garner sat on the small double sofa.

'I just moved in. You did well to find me.'

'Well, we are an organisation. That's the whole point of the police, isn't it?'

'Yeah, I guess. I wouldn't know.'

'No, of course not.'

Williams looked around the room.

'Nice place you have here. An improvement on your last flat, I take it. You had a bit of luck a while ago, didn't you? So I hear. And then a bit of bad luck. But that's gambling for you, I suppose.'

'Yeah, that's not just gambling. It's everything, ain't it? Everything goes like that.'

The policeman nodded.

'I'll be back on top soon,' Garner added.

'Glad to hear it. Very glad.'

'So?'

'I hear you've had very exciting times since you've been in London.'

Garner lit a cigarette and then waved away the issue with the smoke.

'Up and down. Nothing that makes it better or worse than Chicago. But it's a nice town.'

'Oh, yes, it's a fine place. Beats the heck out of Cardiff, that's for sure. Have you had any trouble recently?'

'Trouble? No. Why? Do you recommend it?'

'No, I don't personally, but some people just can't stay away from it. You may have... shall we say, ruffled a few feathers. At least that's what I've heard.'

Garner tried to relax in his chair. He was trying to look unconcerned but his movements felt awkward.

'Have I? Interesting comment. I didn't know I was so influential.'

Williams laughed politely for a brief second. Then he asked,

'Does the name Leonard Dessau mean anything to you?'

'Sure. I didn't know him well. I met him at the Grey Cat. The casino. Somebody shot him outside his house, right?'

'Yes, that's right. You met him on the night he was murdered, if I'm not mistaken.'

'Are you sure this isn't official? It's starting to sound very official.'

'If it was official, I'd have brought witnesses, wouldn't I? And I would have come sooner.'

'Sure. You want some coffee?'

'Thank you. That would be most hospitable. No milk or sugar for me.'

'I take it the same way,' said Garner, standing up and going into the kitchenette. Actually, he wanted the coffee for himself and he also wanted a little distraction while he steeled himself for cautious answers. Williams continued talking from the little sitting room.

'What happened?'

'When?'

'With Dessau. I heard you offered him a lift. You were seen leaving the casino together.'

'How d'you know that? Did you talk to Freddie Mills? He didn't mention it.'

'No, I didn't talk to him. But we have eyes and ears in certain places. Some more than others.'

'Sure, I gave him a ride. To the subway. The tube.'

'Which one?'

'How would I know? I'm a stranger round here.'

'Of course, yes. You couldn't be expected to know. I don't know whether it's different in Chicago but here in London the stations have names. Just thought you might have noticed it. But there again, I can't see a wealthy man getting a tube train back to Hampstead. I couldn't help thinking he could have easily afforded a taxi.'

'Maybe he was tight-fisted.'

'Apparently not. As a matter of fact, he didn't drive. Spent half of his life in taxis. When he couldn't get a lift, that is. And I'm not sure the underground runs that late. As you can see, it's a bit of a puzzle.'

Garner began to protest, but Williams placated him.

'Like I say, I'm not here officially.'

The kettle boiled and Garner made the coffee. There was a pause as he brought it in and sat down. Then Williams began again.

'What did you think of him?'

'Dessau? I hardly knew him. He was OK, I guess. Talked a lot. Don't get me wrong... I'm sorry he's dead, but it wasn't my business. He wasn't either a pal or an enemy of mine.'

'And he didn't give you anything?'

'Give me anything? No, only a headache the way he talked so much. Why would he give me anything?'

'No reason, no reason at all.'

They both looked at their coffees as if waiting for them to cool. There was a silence. Williams leaned forward.

'I hear you told someone you knew the train robbers?'

'You hear a lot of things. Somebody misunderstood me and then shot his mouth off. How would I know them? I haven't been here long enough.'

'Of course you haven't. That's exactly what I would have said. You haven't been here long enough. My snouts tell tales sometimes to get me interested.'

Garner had already learned what a snout was but he didn't think it would hurt to pretend ignorance. Williams explained what one was.

'You mean a stool pigeon? Someone who tells tales for money. Dumps on his pals. Why would anyone listen to one of them?'

'Not exactly what I meant, no. But we're drifting. As you know, some of the train robbers were never caught.'

'Still after Bruce Reynolds, huh? He's really giving you the runaround.'

'No, I don't mean Bruce Reynolds. He's not in doubt. We'll get him sooner or later and put him away. We've got him bang to rights. I mean that we know there were three others who *will* get away. We know their names but we can't touch them.'

'If you can't prove anything, how do you know they're guilty?'

'Not the same thing at all, Mr Garner. You know that. We have excellent information to suggest that they were involved but no solid proof that would stand up in court. Not even prima facie.'

'My heart bleeds for you.'

'Yes, I'm sure. Their shares would have come to about £450,000.'

'Lot of money. Spend all that money on records, you could get Count Basie back in the charts.'

Williams became quietly confidential again as though they were in a public place like a café. He was the opposite of Dessau who had discussed his business in public in a loud voice.

'A year or so ago I set up a deal through an intermediary in South London to have some of that money returned. We recovered a small amount. About £50,000.'

'It was in a telephone box.'

'Oh, you know that?'

'It was in the papers. And the robbery was big news in the States. So, you need more. Why? Is the Queen short of money? You got most of the guys that did it.'

Williams laughed politely.

'It's all politics, Scratch – if I can call you that. Catching the villains is no good if the money isn't found. It makes it look like someone succeeded. And then there are lots of silly tales going round about a Mr Big who planned it all, made a fortune and got away with it.'

'That's what newspapers are for.'

'Yes, but it's a dangerous myth. As long as there's someone out there sitting on a huge pile of Her Majesty's cash, then it looks to the public as though crime does pay – if you're smart enough not to get caught.'

'Which they did.'

'Most of them... Now the name of my intermediary...'

'Freddie Foreman,' said Garner, and then realised he shouldn't have. He should know better than to volunteer information to the police. Williams leaned back in his chair, as if the conversation was taking a different turn.

'You're better informed than I thought. Well, never mind. That's not important now. What's important is that the money is still out there.'

'Not a chance. It'll be spent by now. If not by the crooks, by someone else close to them. A lot of their loot was wasted on being on the run. Same with every big crime. Fake passports, plane tickets, untraceable cars, plastic surgery and stuff. Getting their families flown out with them. Paying people to keep their mouths shut. That's a waste of money. Then having to move again when they don't.'

'Oh, yes. You are well informed about these matters, aren't you? And you're right. Being on the run is an expensive business. But you must remember, the ones I'm talking about never *went* on the run because they had no need to. They aren't living in luxury in Spain. They didn't have to take their families to Mexico or Canada. That money has been invested and we don't know where.'

Garner yawned histrionically and then finished his coffee. He wanted Williams out before Ruby came.

'Well, that's a great story, Frank – if I can call you that. Great story. If someone sends me the money can I keep the bag? Oh, and those elastic bands around the notes: I'd like to keep them. I never know where people are supposed to buy elastic bands from.'

Williams paused for a while and then said,

'I hear a whisper that you've got some inkling of its whereabouts. There's talk of a list. Two lists. And the person who gets them both will cry 'Shazaam' and put them together. But a lot of other people will want to get there too.'

'So what do you want me to do? I don't have it. I don't have any list. I didn't know Dessau. He wouldn't give me any list.'

'Unless there was no-one else to give it to.'

Williams drank some his coffee, then pushed it away from himself and stood up.

'I've taken up a lot of your time, Mr Garner. Thank you for listening to me.'

Garner stood up too.

'Sure. We'll talk again soon. By the way, how did Dessau get it?'

'The list? Oh, you're interested in it now, are you? Well, that I don't know. But he was a bookie and bookies can get very nasty. If somebody owed him money, he might take it – or even get offered it – as collateral.'
'And he'd take it to a nightclub with him?'
'Rather than leave it in his house where somebody might search for it.'
Then he added, as if it were highly significant,
'Or maybe he had only just laid his hands on it.'
'You mean actually in the casino? And he gave it to me? And you were hoping that I would have it. And I would just give it to you. No witnesses.'
'The absence of a witness was for your protection.'
'Sure, it was. How ungrateful of me to think otherwise. Well, I'm flattered you care about me so much, Inspector, but I can't help you. I don't have the list. Of course, you don't believe me. But really, I don't.'
Williams shrugged.
'Well, I might believe you, but let me tell you this, Mr Garner: there are people who won't believe you. And they won't come to see you alone and have coffee with you.'
'If they do, I'll make sure I have cream and sugar in.'
'Yes, well, I suppose that's it. Thank you for listening.'
Garner didn't shake hands with him but he opened the door for him. He had nothing against the policeman. (Criminals don't usually hate the police as much as you might think. They leave that to the university Marxists.) But he couldn't work out whether he was playing a straight game. Naturally, Garner, who trusted nobody, assumed not.
He went to the bedroom to have a lie down until Ruby came. He was still tired for some reason. She would wake him up when she came. But

Ruby came quietly, stayed the night and was gone in the morning. Her presence in his life was as light as a breeze. They didn't talk about her condition. As long as she was with him, she knew everything would be all right.

CHAPTER EIGHTEEN

'Hey Scratch, how are you?' said Tommy. He was well pleased that Scratch would come to find him in front of his mates. They looked well impressed. They might even have thought that Tommy had invented Scratch. What? A bloody Chicago hoodlum? And he's a mate of yours? Yeah, sure, Tommy. Perhaps Tommy had a habit of telling such stories. And here he was, looking every bit as convincing as Tommy had said. They were in the back room of a pub in East London called the Pitcher of Rum. There was a sign outside with a picture of an eighteenth-century pirate, although the building was redbrick from 1902.

Tommy introduced his three fellow bandmembers. And if they weren't Bob, Rob and Richard then they were something similar. They were pretty much of a muchness. Whether they were preparing for a practice session or an actual gig was not easy to tell. There wasn't anyone there to watch them and there didn't seem to be enough instruments to go round. Lying around the room were an acoustic guitar, the beginnings of a drum combo, a mike stand and a small speaker that would have blown a fuse if somebody had plugged a banjo into it.

Garner greeted them all and could see that his reputation had preceded him. He knew that coming down here had made Tommy look cool and good in front of them. He greeted them in a friendly manner. Tonight, he wanted friends and accomplices. (But not too friendly: he didn't want to look too approachable.) They didn't disappoint him: they were impressed. Clearly Tommy had passed on all the tales concerning his buccaneering adventures. His visit was big medicine.

'They're all good guys,' said Tommy about his bandmates. 'And they all know how to keep their mouths shut.'

All the lads nodded enthusiastically.

'That's good,' said Garner. 'There ain't nothing worse than a stool pigeon. Worst things I ever seen in my life happened to stoolies.'

They didn't dare ask for details.

'Need a word, Tommy,' said Garner. 'In private.'

He clapped Tommy on the shoulder as if they were comrades-in-arms from way back.

'No problem,' said Tommy.

Garner took Tommy into the public bar, sent him to get the drinks – a scotch for Garner, a pint for Tommy - and then again, told him to keep the change from a pound note.

They both said cheers and took a swig. Then Garner said,

'Money feels good, don't it?'

He was laying on the Chicago argot tonight.

'Sure,' said Tommy. 'It's the cause of a lot of wrong too.'

'Good point, Tom. That's cos it ain't spread out properly. Anyhow, I never met anyone who hated it enough to refuse it.'

(Although he thought of the old man in the café as he said it.)

'It's handy stuff, that's for sure,' said Tommy.

Garner laughed heartily.

'Handy stuff, I like that. You remember how I told you how I started doing...little jobs, shall we say?'

Tommy nodded slowly.

'I remember one job I did. I was your age. It was for a guy called Big Walter. He had a lot of money bet on something once. Doesn't matter what. But he was a clever guy like me. He knew that you didn't sit around waiting for fortune to deal you a glad hand. He knew that the best way to beat the odds was to have inside information. You follow me?'

'Sure. Like them inside traders in the City. They talk about free market competition and then they rig the system from the inside.'

'Exactly. You're a smart kid, Tommy. You're gonna go places like me. You understand everything. Catch on right off the bat.'

Garner took another drink. Tommy was bursting with curiosity.

'Well, this guy, Big James…'

'You mean Big Walter.'

'Sure, that was his name, Big Walter James. Well, he needed someone to go to a bookies after dark and do a little…er…investigating for him.'

'And you did it?'

'Best thing I ever did. It was my first big break. He gave me a hundred bucks. Doesn't sound like a lot now but believe me, I'd never seen such a load of dough.'

'What did you do with it?'

'You wouldn't believe me if I told you.'

'I can't guess.'

'Promise you won't laugh at me?'

'Oh Scratch, come on…'

Laugh at Scratch Garner? The thing was inconceivable.

Garner leaned forward confidentially.

'I gave it to my mother.'

'Your mother? You're joking!'

'Sure, why not? What do you think I did it for? Drugs? We needed the dough at home.'

'For rent?'

'For rent, for food. Things were tough in them days. Like I say, it was my first big break. Took me a lot of courage to do that. I thought I was gonna let him down, you know... chicken out. But I did it. And I never looked back.'

Tommy was silent. Garner leaned back and drained his whiskey.

'And now,' continued the American, 'I've got a big deal coming up. Bigger than anything I've had on for a while.'

He leaned forward again for the close.

'And I need that inside information. I didn't think I was gonna be able to find someone who had that courage, who had what it takes. But I figure you're my guy on this.'

He took his hand out of his pocket, and put something under a beer mat. Then his slid it towards Tommy. Tommy looked at it.

'Go ahead. Take a peek.'

Tommy lifted up the beer mat. There was £50 underneath.

'That's just the beginning, Tommy. Just the beginning,' said Garner, as he outlined what he wanted Tommy to do.

CHAPTER NINETEEN

As Garner came out of his flat the next day, he was not best pleased to see that his doorway had been blocked in by a small yellow Morris Minor van. It was a commercial sort of van but unmarked. He was just about to swear at the heavens when an attractive young woman came skipping out of the house next door. She was wearing a green mini dress with a matching hat and black kinky boots. The shiny boots matched her long black hair. The Carnaby Street Special for this week.
'Oh hi,' she said, chirpily. 'Oh, I'm so sorry. Have I blocked you in? I'll move it right away.'
'You American?'
'That's right!' she said brightly. She sounded like a Mormon cheerleader.
'Now don't tell me! You're from New York.'
'Uh-uh. Chicago.'
'Well, I could see you had the Big City look.'
'You the Midwest?'
'Thereabouts.' They both laughed. 'My name is Jenny. Jenny Leadbetter.'
'Nice,' he said, although he would have sworn she looked Italian.
'Don't worry about the van. I'll move it in a trice. I'm at the wrong address anyway.'
'You selling something?'
'Well, I'm a fashion student really, but I sell cosmetics on the side to pay the bills.'

She laughed. 'Sometimes it does, and sometimes it doesn't.'
She moved her head to one side and then to the other as she said each clause.
'Yeah, I know that one,' said Garner amiably.
She examined the situation in the street forlornly. She could see that her van was now blocked by someone else.
'Oh shoot! I'm not sure I can move it now.'
She tossed him the keys and he caught them.
'How are those famous male visuo-spatial skills of yours?'
Garner smiled at her.
'I don't know what they are but I'll give it a shot,' he said, climbing into the van.
He didn't see whoever was hiding in the van, but whatever it was they used to hit him was very well chosen and highly effective. He didn't see the woman in green climb into the van beside him. He was out cold. While he was asleep, he had a little dream. He was dreaming more and more these days.

'Hey! Scratch, my good friend. Sit down.'
Garner was a little uncertain about being called to the office of Jake 'Chicago' Sommers. He was notoriously reclusive and almost never saw anyone, unless they were either important or in trouble. In trouble with Jake Sommers, that is.
There was another man in a good suit standing by Jake's desk. He looked dangerous. You always need a second-in-command who does

the hatchet work. It leaves the leader free to do politics and to make contacts.

'How you doin', Jake?'

'I'm doin' good. But I don't recall ever being called Jake by someone like you.'

'I'm sorry, Mr Sommers.'

Sommers had a strangely high voice for someone who looked so influential. He turned to a TV set which was showing a news report.

'What d'you think of them Beatles, Scratch? British, aren't they? Place is going to the dogs over there. I was in England after the war. Country was bankrupt. Everything rationed. Black market was a goldmine. Look at those guys. Worse than damn beatniks. I blame the Marshall Plan.'

He paused to light a match for a cigar the size of a policeman's nightstick. Garner thought that the man standing next to him might light it for him, but he didn't move. He didn't light people's cigars, not even for Jake Sommers. He looked like he thought he was as important as Jake Sommers. Garner wondered if Sommers was going to get a knife in his back one day.

Sommers puffed at the cigar while looking suspiciously over the flame and smoke at Garner, as though Garner might be General Marshall. It took a while. He knew how to light a cigar properly. He blew out the match and then let out a long stream of smoke before beginning.

'Good, now Mr Wilson Garner, I don't want to get us off on the wrong foot. I like you. There may be opportunities for you in my organisation. That's depending, of course. All depending on you. How you behave, how you perform and so on. That make sense?'

Garner nodded, although it made little sense to him. He was in his forties. Nobody important had ever noticed him before.

Sommers carefully nudged the ash from his cigar into an ashtray.

'I have a little errand for you. Do this for me and there'll be some money in it. Do it good and there could be other small services you could do for me.'

'You can depend on me, Mr Sommers.'

Sommers looked at him as if to say, 'Really?' Then he spoke again.

'That's good. Now take this little package over to a man called Tony. It's money, Scratch. Now Tony lives down over in the Loop. He's expecting you. The address is there. Read and then burn it. Then when you come back, we can talk.'

'I'll do that, Mr Sommers,' said Garner and suddenly he was no longer in Sommers' line of sight. He stood up and left with the package.

'You trust him with that?' said Bernie, Mr Sommers' associate. 'A man like that? You'll never see that dough again.'

'I know, I know. You must learn, Bernard, that in life some people are both useful and expendable,' said Sommers.

'Some people are useful because they are expendable,' he added.

He stubbed out the hardly smoked cigar. Cuban cigars were illegal in the United States and Sommers had hoped that the flavour would be improved by its being forbidden fruit. He was disappointed. But then, he was a notoriously hard man to please.

Garner awoke with a strange feeling. He felt as though he were hanging upside down. As his mind cleared, aided by a bucket of water being thrown at him, he realised that this was because he *was* hanging upside down. The bucket hadn't been cleaned in a while and it wasn't drinking water. He could see a large chain suspended by a hook in the ceiling. The chain was wrapped around his feet. This was what was holding him up. He hoped it was a strong chain.

As he started to focus, he could see that there were three men in the room. One, standing impassively off to the side, had his arms folded over a sawn-off shotgun. He would take no part in the cabaret that followed.

The other two were a sight to behold. If Edgar Allen Poe had invented or designed Laurel and Hardy, then they would have looked like this. One of them, like some hellish corpulent uncle from a horror story, was straddled grossly over a backwards dining chair. He was picking his teeth nonchalantly. The other who was standing next to him looked as though he had died of consumption sometime in the 1920s and risen recently from a stone tomb at sunset.

They were all Americans, he could tell that. This was not a good beginning to the day. The gaunt one who was standing took another bucket of foetid water and threw it again at Garner, making sure to soak his entire body.

'Good,' said the avuncular man. 'Mr Garner has re-joined us. Now we can begin our little symposium.'

He was in his shirt sleeves. The gaunt man was wearing a suit he seemed to have bought at two separate jumble sales. The avuncular man looked at his toothpick and then continued.

'You know who we are, Scratch? Or should I say, you know whom we represent?'

He waved his toothpick at his thin companion.

'Grammar, you see. Whom.'

The gaunt man nodded.

'Whom,' he repeated. He clearly enjoyed the educational aspects of his job.

'Now, lookey here Scratch… when you left the United States in such an unseemly hurry all those months ago, you took something that didn't belong to you. It belonged to a friend of ours who had entrusted you with the safe keeping of said item. Am I right?'

Garner said nothing.

'Wake him up a little more, Gomo,' added the avuncular one, still fascinated by his toothpick.

The gaunt man, Gomo, carefully filled the rusty bucket from a tap and then threw it all over Garner again. Then he picked up an electric prod from the floor and zapped Garner with it. Garner had no choice but to scream.

'That's good,' continued the spokesman. 'I want your undivided attention, Scratch. I don't want you dreaming in class. Now, you know why we're here. There was a most unseemly mix-up about this whole affair. Some money going missing and people accusing other people of pretending that they never received said money when they did and I don't know what. Things were said which people no doubt later regretted. Why, I'm not exaggerating when I say that it nearly started a gang war. In fact, if I'm not mistaken, a man called Tony reaped a terrible vengeance over the confusion. They thought *he'd* stolen the money.'

The man chuckled and shook his head.

'Imagine that!' he said amiably. 'What a mix-up! And all the time, Scratch, *you* had the money.'

Garner had to say something, so he swallowed an uncomfortable upside-down swallow and said,

'Look, I've had some luck recently. And I'm in line for some more. I can get the money back to Big Jake.'

'Well, that's nice,' said the man who was doing all the talking. 'I'm very pleased for you. It's nice to have some luck in life. Life can be very hard-edged sometimes. Why the tales I could tell you! But I'm afraid, Scratch, that you just don't get it.'

He waved his instructional toothpick again at the man from the grave.

'He doesn't get it, Gomo.'

Gomo shook his head sadly. It was a shame, he seemed to be thinking. You could tell that he had hoped that Garner would get it and that then they could all shake hands and go home. All this unpleasantness might have been avoided.

'How can I explain this?' said the sitting man languidly. He paused to gather his thoughts, then continued.

'The other day, my boy – he's about seven – stole a cookie after my wife had specifically said that he couldn't have one. Well, she chased him down the street and brought him back to the house – and my goodness, didn't she give him such a whipping.'

He chuckled handsomely again at the thought. Gomo smiled. He had never heard such a lovely story.

'Well, now lookey here, Scratch. See, this is the point: by the time she'd caught him, he'd eaten the cookie. Now, do you think my wife chased him so she could get the cookie back?'

Gomo stared in rapturous expectation. He couldn't wait to find out how the cookie story ended.

'No, indeed,' the fat man laughed. 'Why, do you think we couldn't sustain the loss of one cookie? Do you think it was the cookie that mattered? No, see Scratch, she was concerned for his welfare. She didn't want him to grow up to be any sneak thief.'

Gomo shook his head sadly, amazed at all the evil in the world.

'We want our boy to grow up respectable. Go to college. Be a credit to us. Not like us. We had to cut corners to survive when we were young, didn't we, Gomo?'

Gomo agreed, but you could see he was ashamed of the memory.

'But those times have passed and the world has changed.'

Gomo nodded wisely. A college education. A fine thing.

'She punished him for his own good,' continued the wise old owl. 'She didn't think that a good hiding would bring the cookie back. And of course, I have other kids. His punishment had to be an example to them. And the truth is, Scratch, I, and the parties we represent, care about your moral welfare. We really do.'

Gomo could not have agreed more. He cared. He really cared.

'We don't want back the peppercorn change that you stole. We want to make sure that you and others in our employ grow up wise and respectable, see?'

He nodded to Gomo, who hit Garner with the prod again. Less surprised by the pain, he tried not to scream, but he only just managed it. Instead, he made a noise like a faulty waste-disposal unit.

'Talk to me, Scratch,' said the man, ever fascinated by his toothpick. 'Don't ignore me. It's an offence to my sense of self-esteem. It makes me all...'

He searched for the *mot juste*.

'Alienated,' said Gomo, with a voice from beyond the grave.

'Good,' said the big man, pleased at his protégé's progress. 'Good word. Alienated. It makes me all alienated. And then I just can't *think* straight. I get all confused and irascible. You know, I find that people don't like me when I'm alienated. It seems to bring out the worst in me. No doubt that's a vice and I need to attend to it.'

He nodded decisively to Gomo who nodded back imperceptibly.

'What do you want me to do?' grunted Garner. The man slapped his thigh in joy.

'Excellent! Now we're communicating. Now he's listening, Gomo. My job is to educate people. I can't educate those who are obtuse or surly.'

He nodded to Gomo. Gomo took up a huge blackjack from his collection of goodies on the floor and hit Garner in the stomach. Then he moved around him, choosing his spot correctly and hit him in the kidneys with the end of the cosh. Then he started punching him less judiciously in various other places. Garner tried not to shout. He was naturally stubborn, but self-restraint was not a skill he had spent much time developing. He was worried he would bite through his tongue.

Pausing for breath, Gomo said,

'May I kill him now?'

'In good time, Gomo. In good time. Yes, we will kill him. But he must carry the mark of shame on his body. Now what's that phrase? *Pour encourager les autres?* My French wasn't ever too good.'

He signalled to Gomo to continue his work. Gomo hit Garner again and again. He was good at hitting people. He knew exactly where to hit them. Garner began to wonder whether death might not be a blessed release. Gomo paused for breath. He wasn't smiling but he was happy in his work. He turned and appealed to his companion.

'Excellent, Gomo, excellent. A little more and then you may kill him.'

'Nobody's getting killed on my manor,' said another voice that was not American. This was a solid South London voice. It belonged to a stocky and vicious-looking, bespectacled man of about thirty-five. He spoke very softly – and without a doubt carried a very big stick. Although Garner wasn't in a position to make accurate assessments, he could see that this was the man lurking in the shadows in the photo.

The man seated astride the chair, stood up for the first time.

'Now wait a minute, sir! We had a deal.'

'And you've been paid. You found your man and you've given him a kicking. Job done. Now you can get lost. Nobody gets shot on my manor - not unless I put out the contract. I have a good understanding with the police round here. We know the rules and we don't break them. That way we get to go about our unlawful business without interference.'

'Sir, this is a mere detail that can be negotiated,' said the big man. 'We wouldn't dream of embarrassing you in your home circuit. Why that was understood from the beginning, wasn't it, Gomo?'

But Gomo was too emotional to speak. His heart had been broken by the knowledge that there would be no killing today.

'You're not gonna top him,' said the Englishman.

The big man arranged his thoughts.

'Sir, we represent a party who appreciates good and fair business practice as much as he deplores double-dealing and duplicity. Why, like your good self, he understands the importance of keeping the rules. I suppose you could say it's why we're here.'

'Nobody's double-dealing. You've had your fun, now bugger off. And tell your friend there with the sawn-off not to get any fancy ideas. I've got five blokes here and we're all carrying.'

Gomo looked pained and puzzled, as though the secret of life were just out of reach of him.

Even from his difficult position and in the dim light, Garner could see that two of the five were the boxer and the trilby. But they didn't say anything this time. The large American considered for a minute and then said,

'This, sir, will go badly.'

'So will you if you don't get out. I told you, no killing. We've had enough of that for one year,' he added, glaring at the boxer. The big American man said nothing for a while. Then he jerked his head and he and his two accomplices left. Gomo was close to tears.

The bespectacled man walked around the garage for a while and then looked at Garner.

'Cut 'im down. He's gone a funny colour. He's clashing with the décor.'

Two of his accomplices found a step ladder and slowly let Garner down. He collapsed in a heap on the filthy, oil-stained floor. The bespectacled man threw him a hipflask and Garner swallowed a good deal of the contents. He wasn't too sure what was in it, but it was liquor. The man watched Garner for a while and then spoke in his soft voice.

'You must like crawling around on the ground, the people you upset. Yeah, I know…it was all a misunderstanding.'

Garner offered him the flask back, but the man waved at him to keep it.

'If you're going to live like this, Scratch, you should employ a stunt man. You know who I am?'

Garner knew all right, but he shook his head.

'You do, but I'll tell you. My name's Freddie Foreman.'

Foreman sat down on the chair that had recently been vacated. It was almost impossible to hear him, he spoke so quietly.

'You'll like me,' he continued. 'I don't want blood like that freak show does. I like money. Don't get me wrong: I'm not saying I can't get nasty. I can be very nasty.'

'So those two belong to you?' asked Garner, finding his voice at last. He waved his hand towards his two previous acquaintances. Even waving at them caused him pain and he winced.

'These two cretins?' said Foreman. 'Not exactly, no. They're not my boys, but they are assisting me in a difficult case. They've been sent by someone else. What they call a merger in the City. You see, you've upset a lot of people, Scratch. There's a lot of interested parties.'

'They pushed my car in the river.'

'You were lucky. Somebody wanted to push *you* in the river. Some people wanted the car chained to your ankle when it went down. You see, there's a bit of a conflict which we're trying to resolve here. Some people want you warned off, some people want you to find it. And some people want you going for a swim in the Thames. Me? I'll be happy just to find what I'm looking for. But I'd better bloody find it. Now where is it?'

'Where's what?'

'Now you're a long way into this, Scratch. Let's not go back to the beginning. Where is it?'

Garner said nothing.

'Do you know what makes me angry, Scratch? You'll laugh at this... When people ignore me. Don't make me ask again. Where is it?'

Garner said nothing.

'Now be sensible, Yank. I'm not like those nutters. You couldn't negotiate with them. They were just after a pound of flesh. There was nothing you could give them. I just want an item that is mine and not yours. You can walk away from here in one piece and we can even be mates and have a drink sometime. But I will get it.'

'My bank has it,' said Garner, after a pause.

'Good. Now we're getting somewhere. Do you know, Scratch, if you're not careful, I might believe that beating they gave you was all worthwhile. Now, is that the truth?'

'Seriously, it's with my bank. It's in a security box.'
'Good. And what are you going to do now, if I let you go?'
'Go and get it.'
'And...?'
'Give it to you. Take the damn thing. I don't want it anymore. I'm sick of the trouble it brings.'
Garner felt the wounds on his body one by one. There was a lot of them.
'You're going up in my estimation, Scratch. I thought you was a moron. That was based on the evidence available to me at the time. But you're a man who learns from experience. Aren't many of them about these days. Now there's just one thing. You might get the idea that if you walk out of here, you don't have to deliver on your promise. That would mean you're *not* a man who learns from experience. And my judgment would have been wrong. And that would be an embarrassment for me. I don't like being embarrassed. That's an English thing. You Yanks wouldn't understand it. We just don't like being embarrassed over here. You see my problem?'
Garner heaved himself painfully up from the floor. No-one helped him.
'No, really, I'm serious. I'll get it back to you.'
'Yeah.' Foreman nodded. 'Judging by what's just happened, how difficult do you think it would be for me to track you down?'
'Not difficult. Easy.'
Garner took another swig from the flask. He coughed his guts out. His whole body was in revolt.

'Very. If you try and get a passport or a plane ticket, I'll know about it. Tell me Scratch, what are the chances of a man with a face and voice like yours melting into the background of English society?'

'Zero.'

Foreman nodded slowly.

'Zero,' he said. 'Your middle name...Now listen Scratch. Somebody trusted you once. In Chicago. But it turns out, that they trusted you to do the wrong thing, the bad thing. The trouble that you caused, they wanted caused. But as you can see, that doesn't make you a hero to them. If I don't get that list from you, Scratch, I won't do anything. I'll simply hand you straight back to those pirates who just had you. And I'll let them do whatever they want with you. Are we communicating?'

'Yes.'

Foreman waved his hand at the garage door.

'It's midday now. You've got until tomorrow at noon. Twenty-four hours. You know where I am. Everyone knows me. And you know everyone who knows me.'

Garner walked to the door of the garage. Doing that was enough pain to be going on with. He went outside. He wasn't sure where he was, but it wasn't the West End. He hoped he could find a taxi soon.

CHAPTER TWENTY

Garner needed a break. He told himself that he needed space to take stock. He was still kidding himself that time spent staring at the table or into space was thinking. At any rate, he needed to relax for a night, somewhere where nobody could find him. Somewhere where his wounds could heal. Somewhere where the fluttering of moths against the window wouldn't make him start. He needed one night alone with a bottle, somewhere where he could let his guard down. One night of oblivion.

At home he undressed and examined the damage. His body was a mass of bruises. His torso looked like a bad banana. The sight of himself in the mirror made him run to the bathroom and throw up, although that could have been the aftershock. He rested for a while. He was in one of those states where you want to lie down when you are standing up and you want to stand up when you are lying down. He heaved himself up, dressed again, slowly, and left the flat.

He walked a very laboured walk a long way towards the centre of London. He walked until he was sure that nobody was following him. He stopped at an off licence to invest in a supply of anaesthetic for the night. He walked slowly and painfully until his strained muscles insisted on transport. Then he hailed a taxi. 'Islington,' he said in a loud voice through the cab driver's window. Then when he had got in, he told the driver that he had changed his mind.

'Just take me to a good hotel in the centre,' he said.

The driver took him at his word and drove to the Dorchester. It was the height of the season, but Garner managed to get a cancellation. The price for one night was enough to turn Dale Carnegie white, but Garner didn't care. This was an emergency.

He had no bags with him – leaving his flat with luggage would have aroused suspicion if he was being observed. But he explained to the desk clerk that his wife was having a fashion party that night and he just wanted to be out of his apartment. He winked at the man, as if this would make him think that they were both men of the world who understood each other. The desk clerk just nodded. He could see that Garner was in a state, but he didn't care why he wanted the room. He was off duty in ten minutes and had a date. He was very polite but truthfully, he didn't care if Garner wanted to jump out of the window. And Garner looked very much like a man who wanted to jump out of the window.

The bell boy showed him to his room and dropped a hint that he could provide all sorts of services above and beyond his job specification. Garner told him to get lost but tipped him enough to keep him friendly. He might need an ally later on. And he wanted the boy to know that if someone offered him a bribe for information concerning the occupant of room 506, he could trump the offer.

Once alone, he took off his shoes and sat on the bed. He took out the bottle of whiskey. Then he took a swallow. And then, about to take another shot of the very thing which he thought he needed to calm his nerves, his nerves failed him. His fear took over. He knew he couldn't get too drunk in case he had to react. Now the evidence of Garner's life was that even when he was as sober as Billy Graham, his ability to master a situation was such that he might just as well have been stoned to catalepsy. But the fear took control of him. He took one last small shot and put the bottle on the bedside table. Then suddenly he looked at the door. He got up and walked slowly over to it. Then he pulled it quickly open. There was no-one there. He went back to the bed, lay down and napped restively for a while. He dreamed vividly about pain. Dreams were new to him, as was the troubled and uneven sleep which allowed them to flourish.

When he awoke, it was late and starting to get dark. He got up and looked out of the window. London was disappearing. By day, it had a character all of its own. By night, it was like any other city: an anthill covered in fireflies. Out there somewhere in that glistening and brooding mass were people who wanted to hurt him. People who hated him enough to kill him. People who wanted to kill him, even though they didn't hate him. It was just their job. Or their hobby. Maybe their calling in life. Or maybe it was just the only thing they were good at, and they clutched at it in desperation to keep themselves sane.

And then suddenly, alone in that safe haven, he began to feel more afraid than before: mainly because he was like a child who had awoken in strange surroundings. He felt a bewildering feeling of being homesick, even though he had no home. Even though he belonged nowhere. Outside, the dark city and its bright lights looked like a starry night sky, a vast universe that he didn't belong to.

It would be an exaggeration to say that he began to come to a moral understanding of himself. Concepts like 'good' and 'bad' were beside the point with a man like Garner. Only survival mattered. But he did begin to develop an awareness of his pitiable smallness in the cosmic context. He came close, very close, to the edge of realising that he could not go on like this. There was a long, long way to go before redemption, but it was a start. If he lived long enough.

It was late. He picked up the bottle and drank some more. He had finished it all before he found the courage to sleep again.

In the morning, of course, he felt awful. The bottle of whiskey had cost him next to nothing. Nonetheless it was the most expensive hangover he had ever had. And he was too sick to eat the luxurious breakfast that he had paid for. Sobriety brought more anxiety. The heightened nervousness of a hangover increased the agony of his muscles. And he was back in the real world. He was back in the jungle where the serpents knew his name, address and telephone number. He had wasted more money and bought himself nothing. Instead of buying time, he had squandered it.

He hailed a taxi and went back to his flat for more staring, disguised as thinking. He waited for Ruby to call but she didn't.

Now, all of a sudden, he was in a hurry. That wasn't a problem, as long as he could decide which direction to hurry in. The options were: firstly, give Foreman the list. Most people in his situation would have thought that this was the logical choice and best option. Of course, this would mean that he had £2500 to last him the rest of his life. Having money in the bank should have meant time to think, but somehow it never did. You stared and stared and puzzled and then before you knew it, the time was up and you were a year older, the money was gone and no decisions had been made, because none were obvious or because they involved courage or embarrassment. Or just measly common sense.

The second option was to keep the list and disappear. That meant saying goodbye to Ruby. He would miss her and she would be devastated. She would also be an unmarried mother. It was some comfort to reflect that she might have been better off without him. This thought, masquerading as brutal honesty and self-criticism, was actually a nascent justification for doing a cruel thing.

The third option was to go in with Freddie. Freddie Mills, that is. Help run the club and pool their knowledge about the list. But there was no certainty that Freddie's club would survive, and he might waste the last of his money. He couldn't go home. Not back to Chicago, that is. All exits had been blocked by himself.

All he wanted was the answer to one question. It must have occurred to him that finding the other list would not have solved his problems, and would almost certainly have increased them. But both together, they seemed to be his only salvation. And if he really did have the key to a fortune, he would be able to disappear much more effectively. He turned his tired, agitated mind into chewed cud, churning these thoughts around in his head.

His brain felt the same as his body, as though it had been pummelled and beaten. He knew he had wasted nearly a whole day without purpose. He needed rest badly for body, soul and mind. He would have to be at the bank soon to get the list out and then make his way to Freddie Foreman's place. If he decided to go there.

Where was Ruby? She may have called while he had been in hiding. But he couldn't call her to find out.

Despite all the turmoil inside his head, the decision was made that morning out of sheer animal stubbornness. No longer hanging up by a chain and without any guns trained on him, he simply decided to tell Foreman to go to hell. Not only that, but his kidneys hurt where they had taken punishment from Gomo. He was aching all over and it didn't help with his calm assessment of his situation. He felt a burning resentment, oddly enough, against the man who had released him.

He would find the other list. There were other people he could talk to. Well, at least one. It might have been better for him if there were no options left. But he had come so far now, he only had one more person to talk to.

Finding out where Ronnie Knight lived might have been difficult, but finding out where celebrities live is a little easier. Barbara Windsor was in the phone book. Truly, these were still innocent times.

If he could just get the answer to one question, then he was set. Who knew, he might even be able to do a deal with Freddie Foreman when he had both lists. After all, wasn't that what he wanted? And hadn't he said himself that it was money not violence that he was interested in?

He went to the bank and retrieved the list. Then he set off for Knight's place.

Barbara even opened the door herself when he rang the doorbell. She was wearing a silk patterned dressing gown and had obviously only just got up.

'Miss Windsor? My name is Wilson Garner. You remember meeting me?'

'Oh, yes of course. Scratch, isn't it? You're a friend of Freddie's. Come in.'

He hadn't expected to be invited in. He was really moving upwards.

She showed him into the lounge. It was a nice house but not too big or showy. She was famous now but only at the beginning of a long career. She motioned to him to sit on the chintz sofa and sat on a chair herself.

'Are you all right? You don't look very well.'

'I'm fine. I won't take up too much of your time.'

'You're lucky to find me at home. I'm normally up early working. I haven't got long though: I'm off for a photo shoot in an hour. Takes me that long to get ready.'

She leaned forward and giggled as she said it.

'No problems, Mrs Knight...'

'Call me Babs.'

'Thanks. My business is very short...Babs. I have only one question.'

He pulled out the photo. It was starting to look a bit tatty.

'I'm sure you remember this occasion.'

She looked at the photo. He tried to read from her face what she was thinking, but she betrayed nothing. He was some card player.

'Oh yeah. Vaguely. I go to so many places.'

'I can imagine. You must be in demand.'

Garner was straining to be charming, but it was too late in the day to be learning new skills.

'Was there some sort of competition there? Like lifting this barbell?'

'What a strange question. Not that I remember.'

'Don't tell me. It was all for charity. It was all just a joke. No serious competition took place.'

'Well, if that's what other people have told you, Scratch, and that's what I tell you, well...that's all there is to say.'

Suddenly, Garner lost it. It was miraculous that he hadn't done before now.

'And you were only there to help out and get photographed!' he shouted. 'And you only 'popped in' for fifteen minutes and you don't know what the hell I'm talking about.'

"Ere, I don't like your tone. What's going on? Ronnie!'

But Ronnie was already there. He was standing on the staircase in a towelling robe. His hair was wet.

'What's going on? What do you want with my wife?'

'The answer to one question. I thought it was a simple one. But it seems to be the hardest question in the world.'

'Maybe you should ask Einstein. You've had your answer – now get out.'

He came all the way down the stairs. Garner was bigger than he was.

'I hear on the grapevine you've had a good drubbing recently. Well deserved, I should think and probably the first of many. No, not the first. Not by any means. Sticking your nose all over the place. Pestering the wrong people.'

Garner stood up.

'Tell me who would be the right people to pester?'

Knight turned to his wife.

'You'd better get ready, Babs.'

She stood up and said,

'I don't want any trouble, Ron. Just tell him to go.'

'Don't you worry, baby; I'll be fine. You go and get ready.'

She left the two men alone.

'Now, let's you and me have a little talk, Scratch.'

Garner sat down again and Ronnie took the chair that his wife had vacated. He stared at Garner for a few seconds.

'You all right? You look bloody terrible,' said Knight.

Garner nodded. He felt it was time he took the initiative.

'Every time I talk to someone, they all say the same things. They all hear the same things on the grapevine. There's something buzzing around here and I'm the only one who isn't in on it. They all seem to know my business but I can't get anyone to open up to me.'

'You're an outsider, Scratch. It takes time to be accepted in a little closely knit world. If I'm not mistaken, you belonged to a similar world in the States. You were asked to run a little errand. For someone in Chicago. I don't know the details – no, no, I'm not making any judgments. We've all got our dark little corners in our lives – but you're a loose cannon, Scratch. An uncertain entity – and trust is everything in the shadow world.'

Garner showed him the photo.

'Yeah, I seen it in the local rag.'

He turned it over and looked on the back.

After a pause he said,

'Maybe it doesn't mean physical strength.'

Garner leapt on this opening.

'That's what I figured. Could be a strong personality like Diana Dors. But she wouldn't tell me anything.'

'No, she wouldn't get pushed around easily. You wouldn't get much change out of her. Maybe, it means Freddie Foreman. You know, strong as in powerful. Why don't you go and pester him?'

'No need: I met him.'

'Yes, so I hear.'

'I'm pretty sure he doesn't have it, otherwise he wouldn't be after me to give it to him.'

There was a pause. If Knight knew that there was also a second list which Foreman would also have wanted, he didn't say anything.

'Listen, you're a bit of a buffalo at a tea party but you're all right, Scratch. Now, look, I hope that you do the decent thing, the smart thing. I really do. But somehow, I just know that you won't. I just know that you'll do the wrong thing. The dumb thing.'

Knight stood up and gave him the photo back.

'We can't help you. Nobody can help you. Don't come back here and don't pester my wife again. You may be a big guy Scratch, but you're on enemy territory without a map. Somehow, I think you might be better off trying to find the *weakest* person. Your body would be better off.'

He waved his hand upwards to tell Garner to get up. Garner heaved himself out of the chair.

Knight showed him to the door. There was nothing to be gained by staying any longer. Garner made to leave.

'One more question, Scratch,' said Knight.

'You want to ask me a question, but I can't get a straight answer from anyone.'

'Have you spoken to everyone in that photo?'

'I think so, yes. I've eliminated everyone I think might be the strongest.'

'You want some really good advice, Scratch? Tear that bloody thing up and forget it.'

'I'm too far in. Listen, we don't have to fall out, Ronnie.'

'Nor do I want to. But if you come back here pestering my wife again, I'll have ten guys on you. And they won't hang you up by your feet, mate.'

Garner nodded slowly and looked at the photo. Knight stared at him. For a moment it looked as though he really was going to tear it up. Then he put it back in his pocket and left. Knight shook his head sadly and closed the door.

CHAPTER TWENTY-ONE

Garner had only been back at the flat ten minutes when the phone rang. He was expecting Ruby, but it wasn't Ruby: it was her father.

'Wilson?'

'Yeah, hi Donald.'

'I don't know whether Ruby has called you, but it's about Tommy.'

'What's going on?'

'I'm not too sure myself. He's been caught breaking into a place.'

'Place? What place?'

'It was a gym somewhere in South London. Near Streatham. What he was doing down that neck of the woods, I don't know.'

'Yeah, I know. That's miles away.'

Donald paused, like a man who was out of his depth. Then he continued,

'I don't know what's got into him recently. All this pop music if you ask me. And he's got money from somewhere too. Buying his friends drinks. New clothes, records. I don't know what's going on.'

'Why would anyone want to break into a gym?'

'I dunno. Nothing makes sense about that boy these days. Whole country's going barmy.'

'Well, I haven't heard from Ruby. Tell her to call me if you speak to her. Anything I can do to help, let me know.'

'Yeah. I was going to say speak to him. He looks up to you, Scratch. But I suppose it's too late now.'

Garner put the phone down and let out a sigh of relief. If Tommy had been caught breaking into the Nightspot, there would have been hell to pay. The trouble could have been traced back to him. He had told Tommy to search Mills' place first. Whatever his reasons for going to Streatham first, Garner wasn't going to argue with them. And as for telling the police anything, he knew he was safe. He had put the fear of death into Tommy about being a stoolie. Of course, Tommy wasn't very bright. The police could trick something out of him.

Ruby called not long after. She hadn't been home yet after the club. She was in a terrible state.

'Oh Scratch! It's about Tommy.'

'Yeah, I heard. Your dad called me. Look don't worry. Kids get into trouble. They won't send him down, I don't think. Not the first time.'

'Oh, but Scratch, it isn't the first time. He's always in trouble.'

'He'll be OK. He'll grow out of it. Are you coming over?'

'Later on. I need to go and speak to my parents. I'll see you later.'

'Have you told them yet? About…you know…'

'Not yet. I was going to when this happened. Oh, Scratch, everything's going wrong. Why is everything going wrong?'

She cried and then suddenly hung up.

She came when he was in bed and climbed in next to him. She tried not to wake him, but his sleep was restive.

'You OK?'

'Yes, Scratch.'

She placed her hand on his chest and nestled close to him. It was too dark for her to see the extent of his bruising.

'Scratch, everything will be OK, won't it? You will stay with me, won't you?'

'Sure. What have I said makes you think I won't?'

'I don't know. I worry. My parents are frantic. I've never seen them in this state. We've never had much but we've never had problems like this until now.'

'Baby, everything will be OK.' He pressed her close. He tried not to let her know how much it hurt to do that.

'As long as you stay with me, I can face it Scratch. But...'

'But what?'

'You never settle. I want to see you settle.'

'I will. I have to settle sometime. Why not now? I just have some business to get right and then I'll be OK. It won't take too long. Then everything will be square.'

'Everybody says that, Scratch. They always have something to do, one thing before they can relax and everything will be fine once they've done that one thing. But there's always another thing...and then another. They keep turning a corner and there's another corner at the end of the road. And there's no end to it until they die.'

'Baby, it'll be OK. I promise.'

'I've never been scared in my life before. And now I'm scared all the time. Scratch, you would tell me if you were in trouble, wouldn't you?'

'Why? Why would I tell you if I was in trouble? Would I be doing you a favour if I did?'

'But I need to know, Scratch. We shouldn't have secrets.'

'OK, you want me to add to your worries? Yeah, I'm in trouble. I'm in a lot of trouble. And you know what? I can get out of it just like that. All I have to do is give up. You want me to give up?'

'I don't know, darling. I don't know what it is. Sometimes I think I don't know anything about you. Give up what?'

'Good question. Give up what? The way things are now, the way the cards have fallen, the cards I still have in my hand – everything. I'd be giving up everything.'

Ruby began to cry.

'I don't understand Scratch. I don't understand what you're saying. I don't understand what situation you're in.'

'No. Me neither. Go to sleep, Ruby,' said Garner. She was hoping he would make love to her, but he went back to sleep. She understood. He was tired. She didn't sleep for a long time and then only fitfully.

CHAPTER TWENTY-TWO

Garner slept in a long time the next day. Ruby had left early. She had written a note in her neat little handwriting saying she had not wanted to wake him, but she had to go back home, what with things the way they were. She said she loved him but wanted to have a little talk with him sometime. When he wasn't too tired. If that was all right.

Garner was tired for sure. He was completely drained. And no amount of sleep seemed to reinvigorate him.

Maybe Knight was right. He had explored and exhausted every avenue now. It was all over. He still had Foreman to deal with, but he could always placate him by handing over the list.

He washed, then went out for a paper and waited for the early cafes to open. Then he planned his day. One of his chores would be to get yet another car. He would put that off for a while. He was spending cash like a government. He wanted a breather from the constant drain of resources.

When he came back to the flat, the phone was ringing. A voice which sounded like a commando with a knife at a sentry's throat said,

'Garner?'

'What do you want?'

'We've got someone here that you know.'

There was a pause and then Ruby's voice came on the line, tremulous with terror.

'Scratch! There are some men here. They won't let me go. They say you've got something they want. Scratch please...help me...'

Her voice went away and then the harsh man came back on the line. You've got until midday, Garner. You know where the Five Star gym is? You were poking your nose around there recently. Don't go in, just wait outside. Someone will meet you there.'

'Wait a minute, what about Ruby?'

'She'll be fine as long as you bring what we want.'

'I'll need time to get it.'

'No, you don't Scratch. You don't need time. All you need is to get smart. That's your only problem. It's a challenge but you could do it.'

'I'm serious. I need to get hold of it.'

'Hey, pretty girl. You hear that? Your boyfriend is playing for time…Midday, Scratch.'

He hung up.

CHAPTER TWENTY-THREE

Garner had a lot to do and little time to do it. He took a cab down to the same car forecourt. The man must have thought he was dealing with a lunatic. This time, all Garner could afford was a small used Ford Popular. The car he had owned originally. He wanted to hold as much liquid cash as he could. The dealer took the money and shook his head.
'Not my job to ask questions,' he said, 'but are you running a demolition derby or something?'
'Funny, but I had the *exact* same idea about it being none of your business. Great minds and all that.'
As Garner drove off the man waved sarcastically and shouted, 'See you same time tomorrow. Buy three cars from us and you get a free Swiss watch.'
Next stop, the Nightspot.
''You're getting to be quite a regular here,' said Mills, as Garner burst into the office. 'Shame you can't always make it when we're open.'
'Never mind the dialogue. Where is she?'
'I don't know what the hell you're talking about, Scratch. Who? Has someone gone missing?'
'Ruby. Ruby Irons. The cigarette girl.'
'Missing? Are you kidding? Good grief, I don't know. I look after my staff like family. I wouldn't see anything happen to her.'
'You'd better be telling the truth, Mills.'
'I swear, Scratch. I may know a few shady characters but I'm not involved in that game. Yeah, I know gangsters. You have to round here.

You can't operate otherwise, just like you have to know the police. Gordon Bennett man, I don't kidnap my own people.'

Garner pulled the photo out again.

'Did you send me that?'

Mills sat down at the desk.

'The truth, Freddie.'

'No, I didn't send it. My partner Andy Ho did. I didn't know anything about it. He didn't know what it meant but he knew that it was a clue of some kind.'

'He figured that I would lead him to the box – or the other list?'

'Whatever. He may have had that idea but personally, I think he greatly overestimated your intelligence. I didn't think you'd have much chance of finding it.'

'What was his interest?'

'Same as yours: he thinks it's money and he wants it. Or should that be 'needs it'. He thought you'd be able to find it. I didn't.'

'But I could ruffle a few feathers, bring a few people out of the woodwork and deflect any attention, right? If I found it, that would be a bonus.'

'Something like that. That was his reasoning, not mine. Maybe.'

'Where is he?'

Mills said nothing. Garner picked up the Chinese box on the desk.

'There's another like this, is there?'

'Yeah. Andy Ho had it. I gave one to a friend, but I gave the wrong one.'

'Deliberately or accidentally?'

Mills said nothing.

'You had one list and Dessau had the other. Where did Dessau get it?'

'The people who had the bank accounts were being watched. He provided them with liquid currency and they gave him that as security.'
'And how did you get involved? Where did you get the second list?'
'One day I'll write my memoirs, Scratch. You can wait until then to hear my life story.'
'Whatever. But you figured it would give you some negotiating power with the loan sharks and mobsters? And you think *I'm* stupid.'
'We're all stupid, Scratch,' said Mills, 'otherwise we'd be in the City, trading bits of paper and living in mansions in the suburbs. I got the crap beaten out of me for a living when I was a boxer. Don't get me wrong, I enjoyed it, met some great people and I got to know what fame is like - but believe me, Scratch, I'd rather have done nuclear physics. Nobody chooses to live like we do.'
'Who did you give it to?'
'You won't get that from me. And anyway, you have another concern at the moment, don't you? Or had you forgotten?'
'It's all part of the same chaos. Who did you give it to, Freddie?'
'Go to hell.'
Garner went round the desk to grab him by the lapels. Perhaps he had forgotten who Mills was. Perhaps he was just making a lot of very poor decisions. Mills was in his forties now, but he had been a great boxer once and was still in decent shape. Garner never stood a chance. Mills was a nice guy, but when it came to fighting he was like a bloody honey badger. He pummelled Garner until he went down. Garner never saw most of the punches. Then Mills picked him up and put him on the chair.
'Sorry, old son. You shouldn't have done that.'

Mills took out his handkerchief and dabbed the blood from Garner's face.

'Forget it,' said Garner. There was some real pain coming from his jaw. He might have fractured it.

'I'm so sorry, but you won't take no for an answer, will you? Come on, you need to get that face looked at. Not to mention the rest of you. And that includes your brain. You're in bloody awful shape, mate. If your life was a boxing match, the ref would have stopped it by now. It's time to throw in the towel, Scratch.'

'Not now: I have to get something. Reach into my jacket pocket. There on the right.'

Mills reached into Garner's pocket and pulled out a cheque book.

'How much do you need?'

Mills was stunned.

'Well, look matey, you're a strange one. First you try to attack me, then I punch your lights out. Now you want to bail me out. I admit I could use some readies, but you need to get to a doctor.'

Mills had no fear of the police if Garner went to the hospital. He knew what kind of man Garner was. It isn't that thieves have honour, but they do have a culture.

Mills lifted Garner up to take him round to the car park.

'No wait,' said Garner, 'I mean it. How much?'

'I don't get you.'

Mills waved his hands uncertainly.

'Fifteen hundred would keep a few dogs away. For a while anyway.'

'Wow, that's a lot of dog food. Write it out. I'll sign it.'

Mills stared at him for a moment and then wrote out the cheque. Then he held it out to Garner.

'Now, listen to me, mate: if this is to get the name of the person I gave the box to, I'll tear it up now. You won't get that from me.'

'I understand. It's not for that. It's a loan, right?'

'Absolutely, mate. Debt of honour.'

Garner reached over and signed with his trademark shaky signature. He had to keep Freddie afloat. He had to keep him onside. If he came back, he would need help. If not, well, perhaps Freddie would bury him.

'I need something else from you.'

'What?' said Freddie suspiciously, as though he had been tricked.

'A gun.'

'A gun? Are you kidding? I don't keep bloody guns. Where do you think you are? This isn't Dodge City. And I'm not an ironmonger either.'

'I didn't think you'd have one, Freddie. But you have contacts. You know where I can get one. I'm in a hurry.'

'Scratch, don't do this. You're way out of your league here. These people are really nasty. All they want is one lousy bit of bloody paper. Give it to them.'

'I can handle myself.'

'Really? Five minutes ago you couldn't handle a middle-aged pug. Give it up, my old mate. It's over. Give them what they want, get married to Ruby and live to a ripe old age of fifty.'

'Give me a name.'

Mills leaned back in his chair. He liked Garner. He didn't know why. He knew he wasn't a good man, but somebody had to like him, and Mills was a forgiving sort.

'All right,' he said. 'I'll give you a name. But I didn't give it to you.'

Garner paused and then picked up the cheque which Freddie had written out. He looked at it for a few seconds and then said,

'That's not your writing on the back of the picture.'

'No.'

'Whose writing is it?'

Mills said nothing.

'The guy you gave the box to?'

'It was just a joke. I asked for a receipt. That was the witty response.'

'Who was it?'

Mills said nothing again, but Garner didn't expect a reply.

'Just give me the name of the supplier.'

Garner listened to the name and address and then staggered out of the club. Mills looked at his watch and got up. The banks were open and he wanted to express the cheque. People change their minds, and he didn't really think Garner was a constant heart.

CHAPTER TWENTY-FOUR

The shop in Peckham didn't appear to be able to make up its mind what it sold. It wasn't exactly a pawnshop. More what you might call a White Elephant Shop. It was full of stuff: some junk and some valuable. Everything was mixed up. If the police ever raided it, the fingerprint man would have a nervous breakdown.

A large man with hair everywhere on his body except where he wanted it, on top, was reading the *Sporting Life*. Perhaps it was busy at weekends. His red-blotched face said he'd had a couple of drinks now and then. He was wearing a large burgundy velvet jacket. A previous attempt to wash it by hand had not been successful. No further attempts at cleaning it had been made.

'Your name Dandy Ken?' said Garner as he entered the shop.

'Never 'eard of 'im,' said the man. 'You must want some other handsome bastard.'

Garner laughed politely. The velvet-clad man kept reading the *Sporting Life*. Garner said,

'A friend gave me your name.'

'Oh dear,' said the man, lowering his paper. 'That's not what friends are for. Friends are people from whom one expects a certain quantum of reticence. The less forthcoming, the more cordiality there is between parties, is what I say.'

'He said you might be able to help me with an item.'

'Help yourself. Have a look around. Everything is either priced or not. If it's not, ask me and I shall make up a price depending on my assessment of your means.'

He took up the paper and started reading again.

Playing the game, Garner looked around and then bent forward, whispering:

'My friend says you can get me a shooter.'

'Did he now?' said the man. He folded up the paper carefully, as if it were a first edition, and placed it on the shop counter.

'I don't think I have one in the window at the moment, sir. Perhaps, you'd like to leave your name and if one comes in, I shall contact you.'

'Listen, my friend, spare me the Vaudeville. I'm in a hurry. I need a gun.'

'Dangerous talk. Dangerous items, guns. Are you sure you got the right man?'

Garner leaned over again and whispered his name. He'd promised Freddie he wouldn't do that. But that was then, and this was now. The man thought for a minute and then got up.

'Did he now? Normally a sensible party. What does he want with sending people on errands like that? A betrayal of trust, that's what I call it. Not conducive to amicability between parties, that's what I say.'

'He doesn't want it; I do.'

The man thought again for a while. He may have been contemplating the issue at hand or he may have been thinking that it was not too early for a swift one out of the bottle under the counter. Eventually, he shook his head.

'No. Don't like it.'

'Why not? I can pay.'

'Why not? Well, there's your accent for a beginning. Americans with guns. Bad mixture. You tend to use them with an alarming readiness. First resort instead of the last. Nor is it good business practice. Guns, my friend, are like Champagne. They're for special occasions. You don't give Champagne to the servants.'

'Yeah? What do your servants drink?'

The man got up out of his chair.

'I have a part time assistant. As an indulgent and modern employer, I provide her with refreshments such as tea bags. Anything more would upset the fine social balance between those party to the employment relationship.'

'You should write for the New Yorker. Now like I say, I'm in a hurry. How much?'

The shop-owner shrugged.

'Well, I can see you are set on your inadvisable path. £300 now. Plus fifty for the ammunition. A man will meet you outside the White Rose pub across the road at three 'o' clock.'

'Yeah? Will he be wearing a white carnation?'

'I very much doubt it, although you could probably grow them under his fingernails.'

'Three pm is too late. I need it now.'

The man shook his shiny head.

'Don't like it. People in a hurry for guns – Americans in a hurry for guns. Not good. It has an unsettling quality about it. A story with a bad ending. Someone will get shot. Names will be thrown about in the pubs and

cafes. Accusations will be made. Now I ask you,' he said tapping Garner's chest, 'will this be conducive to cordiality between parties?'
'Let's make it £400 now.'
'Very well. I can see you are a determined man. My conscience is clear. I have tried to talk you from the dark path. He'll have the gun and the ammunition in an hour. You give him another £150. No, no, please. No handshakes. You colonials are always shaking hands. No rituals are necessary if there is respect between parties, that's what I say. Good day, sir.'
Garner left the shop, grabbed a sandwich from a newsagent's and waited outside the pub. His jaw was killing him. It may well have been fractured if not broken. His kidneys were in pain too. But that could not be a consideration now. He was nothing if not stubborn. The pain would have to wait.
An old man who looked like a Central Park flasher came up to him and showed him the parcel under his filthy mac. He must have bought the coat the same time as he had his last wash. He didn't need a bath, he needed closing down by the health authorities. Needless to say, he said he was expecting £200. Sometimes it worked, and sometimes it got him threatened or assaulted. But this time the gambit was successful for the little man. Garner was in too much of a hurry to argue and he handed over £200. Instead of celebrating his good fortune, the little scrote cursed himself for not asking for more.
Garner looked at his watch. He had about half an hour to get to Streatham. This meant driving fast in a car with a gun in it. He had paid out a lot of money today. He had a lot in his wallet but not much left in

the bank. Mills wouldn't hang about with that cheque, he knew that for certain.

CHAPTER TWENTY-FIVE

The morning had been quite hectic. Garner had had little time to think. He had a gun but had no idea what he was going to do with it. His plan, such as it was, was purely instinctive. But maybe it was more than that. Perhaps, he just wouldn't admit in the front of his mind that he was going to try to have it both ways. He wanted to free Ruby and keep the list. He had no idea how.

He pulled up outside the gym and waited. He had five minutes. He didn't think for one moment that Pallo and McManus were anything to do with this. But some gyms, like some clubs and pubs, are always a haunt for certain types of people.

He waited in his car. Nobody moved. Nobody came. Perhaps it was a trick. Perhaps, he told himself, they never had Ruby at all. They just made her say it and let her go. He wanted to believe that.

Just then, a minicab turned up outside the gym. A woman got out. She told the driver to wait and went into the gym. Garner pulled the dilapidated photo out of his pocket so quickly that he nearly tore it. That was her! The model in the picture. She wasn't wearing her basque and fishnets now, just a white top and brown skirt. But there was no doubt it was she. Diana Dors had been right: she was in her forties. Too old to be a model. Only now he realised that she had been giving him a clue and had sneered at him when he didn't take it. The blonde had wanted the cab to wait, so there was no point in going into the gym. She would be coming out again.

Sure enough, the blonde lady re-emerged and got back into the taxi. She was carrying something. A big pile of books. Were they...? Surely they couldn't be telephone directories? Was this some crazy hallucination? Garner was torn. He knew he had to follow her. He only hoped she wasn't going too far. He had, unbeknown to himself, already softened himself up for the decision. Ruby will be OK, he thought. They won't harm civilians. They just wanted to frighten me into giving up the list, but I have to follow the blonde lady.

There was another consideration too. Several groups of people were after him. If the people who had Ruby were not from Foreman, then giving them the list would not save him from Foreman's wrath. In fact, it would confirm it. He was in a terrible bind. This whole rotten country was becoming too dangerous for him. The only way open to him was forward.

The word 'forward' has acquired cachet in the modern world. People confuse it with progress. Similarly, they think of going back to your starting point as regression. But going back to the start is common sense if you are on the wrong track.

He started the engine and drove off. The cab went a long way and he nearly lost it a few times. Eventually he did lose it. But he had the name of the cab company and a description of the driver. He looked at his watch. It was way too late to go back to the gym now.

Garner stopped at a pub and bought a drink. Then he borrowed a telephone directory and found the cab company. It was local. He went to a booth and called the number. It was over an hour before the cab appeared. Garner went over to the man who rolled down the window.

'How you doin'?'
'All right. You Mr Jefferson?'
'That's me.'
'Where you going? Judging by that face, you need to go to hospital.'
Garner peeled off a tenner from his dwindling bunch of banknotes.
'Never mind my health. I'm insured. I just want some information. You brought a lady here and then took her somewhere.'
'Hang on...what's it to you?'
'I'm a Hollywood talent scout. We want her to play Abraham Lincoln. Where did you take her?'
'I shouldn't really say,' said the driver, looking at the solitary note. Garner peeled off a fiver and added it.
'She went to the airport.'
'The airport?' Garner swore. 'Did she say why? And don't say "to catch an airplane".'
'She's a performer.'
'What kind of performer?'
'Don't ask me, I'm a racing man. D'you want her vital statistics as well?'
'Did she say where she was going?'
'Yeah,' said the driver. 'Copenhagen.' And he drove off.
Garner stared at the cab as it disappeared. There was no choice but to follow the blonde woman. He had spoken to everyone in the photo but her. She must know something. It was time to leave anyway. Everyone was after him in this country and everything was collapsing around him. The only way out was out. Copenhagen. His jaw and his kidneys argued against this decision. They howled for attention. And normally his own

discomfort was something he took very seriously. But this was a bigger emergency. There was nothing else to do and nowhere else to go.

CHAPTER TWENTY-SIX

Garner had a new car – the third car in a few weeks - and now he didn't need it. He drove towards London Airport – later known as Heathrow – and then dumped the car in a side street. It didn't matter if someone stole it. Either he would be coming back in triumph or not at all. Somehow, he knew he was at the turning point. The abyss was in front of him; the sky was above. There was a choice. All he had to do was be able to fly.
Garner had his passport with him. He had everything. He had known it would be too dangerous to go back to his flat for a while. He booked a later flight to Copenhagen, learning from the booking desk that it was the capital of Denmark, a small Scandinavian country to the north of Germany. Garner had no familiarity with European geography. His one chance to learn would have been to join the army during the war but the temporary convenience of a slipped disc kept him stateside. (The booking clerk also told him that Copenhagen was where Hans Christian Anderson was from, and was surprised to find that Garner had never heard of him.)
The seats of the BEA flight were comfortable, but Garner was not. His jaw was killing him; it may even have been broken. His kidneys ached. He could feel the bits that weren't hurting. They felt odd, somehow.
Arriving at his destination, he booked a reasonably priced hotel in the city centre and then went out to explore the place.
Trying to find one person whose name he didn't know in a huge metropolis was something of a challenge. But he did know now for

certain that she was a performer. It could be a simple matter of going round to theatres and clubs. Time, which they say is money, was not on his side. However, in the centre of the city, there was a booking kiosk. He could ask there (his natural assumption being that everyone would speak English). This turned out to be a good move. It is said that things always go smoothly before a disaster.

Next to the kiosk was a gigantic poster presenting Marlene Dietrich at the Tivoli Variety Music Hall. Even Garner had heard of Marlene Dietrich, the great German-American film actress. Underneath was a list of the supporting acts. There was the unpronounceable Preben Uglebjerg, Danish actor and master of ceremonies. Under that name was Bob Williams. Garner had seen him in the States. He was a comedy dog trainer who did a lot of shouting. And then third on the bill for the first half, was Joan Rhodes, *Staerk Dame fra England*. And next to it was a picture of the blonde woman.

You didn't have to be Noam Chomsky to know that 'dame fra England' meant 'lady from England'. But as a man of little learning and even less intellectual curiosity, Garner did not speculate upon the meaning of the word 'staerk', which was unfortunate, as this might have saved him some trouble.

The show began at half past seven, which gave him less time than he thought as Denmark was an hour ahead. He went back to the hotel to take stock. He tried not to think of Ruby.

After the two cars, the flat, the gun, the loan (loan?) to Freddie Mills, the flight and the hotel – oh, and not forgetting the huge loss at cards - he was down to his last few hundred pounds. If this blonde lady were not the key to the mystery, then he was in serious trouble. He might be in serious trouble anyway. Of course, he did have a gun. He had managed to get it into Denmark. It was a lot easier to smuggle a gun on board a plane in the sixties. This was before the age of terrorism and hijackers. Security at both airports had been very lax. Garner had managed to convince them that he had no Swiss watches or perfume in his luggage, and they had seemed satisfied with that. He looked suspicious, as though he had been in a fight, which of course he had. But they waved him through. He had told them he was a boxer and they had believed him. (After all, he hadn't said he was a good boxer.) It was his last piece of luck. You can always rely on luck to get you to your doom.

He sat there in his hotel room for a long tIme nursing the gun as his only comforter. It was a Colt, a small, weedy looking thing. Guns are supposed to be big and powerful, to give you confidence and to frighten people. Despite his background, he had not yet learned that guns cause more problems than they solve. It was just him and the gun, his wits and a few thousand krone. An unbeatable combination. His jaw throbbed sometimes and screamed at others, but luckily he had the pain in his kidneys to distract him. He looked at his watch. He wanted to get to the show before it started. He wanted to talk to the blonde woman.

He must have dozed off. Suddenly, there was a knock at the door. In his nervous state it felt like someone going through a plate glass window and he jumped. He pushed the gun into his waistband. He opened the door slowly but the two men pushed against it and sent him flying. Then they were in. They closed the door behind themselves. It was his old friends, the boxer and the man with the trilby, who seemed to have found his hat again. The boxer took out a knife.

'Well, well, if it isn't Babyface Garner,' said the trilby.

'If I had a baby looked like him, I'd drown it,' said the boxer.

'How the hell did you find me?'

'You were supposed to be outside the gym. We was waiting. We saw you go after that cab. And being curious sorts of souls, we just couldn't help but track it down the same way you did. The driver said you was very generous to him.'

The boxer chipped in with,

'His information didn't cost us nothing.'

'How did you get here? I got the last plane to Copenhagen for two hours.'

'You got the last direct plane. We had to change at Frankfurt.'

'And now we're all tired and upset,' added the boxer. 'Because of you, Scratch.'

'You ever been to Frankfurt, Scratch?'

'Don't bother,' said his echo.

'I don't recommend Frankfurt, Scratch. It's like one big bloody kitchen.'

'We didn't want to be in Frankfurt. We wanted to be at home with our families. But here we are, because of you, Scratch.'

Trilby wiped the perspiration from his neck with a handkerchief.

'Frankfurt is hell designed by Terence Conran, Scratch.'

The boxer nodded as if he had never heard a truer word spoken. But trilby was the only man in the room who knew who Terence Conran was.

'And now,' he continued, 'here we are in Denmark. Nothing to offer the world but bacon, pastries and pornography. Now what am I going to take home as a present for my wife and kids?'

'Where is it?' said the boxer.

'Where's Ruby?'

'Ruby? Listen to Sir Galahad. What do you care about Ruby? You just ran off, all speedy like. You saw them pound signs and off you went to Copenhagen. And now here we all are.'

'Yeah,' said the boxer. 'Where is it?'

Garner stood up looking tired.

'All right you guys. You win. Is Ruby safe?'

'Listen to him! Is Ruby safe? She's all right,' said trilby, 'but no thanks to you. We just wanted her to help throw a scare into you. But she knows you now, Scratch. We had her in the car. She saw you drive off. And you the father of her child.'

'She knows now,' echoed the boxer. 'She knows you don't care about no-one except Scratch Garner.'

'That was our miscalculation,' said the trilby. 'We just assumed you was a square bloke. We'll know better next time. Like Ruby. Our New Year's resolution is to be all suspicious-like in future. Now where is it?'

'It's right here,' said Scratch. He put his hand towards his pocket but then drew out the gun. He didn't have time to think and probably wouldn't have anyway. He shot the trilby. He shot the boxer too, but not before the big man had had time to stab him in the leg. (Clearly, no-one trusted the boxer with guns anymore.) Garner was no expert with firearms but they were too close for him to miss. They were both dead.

Garner stared for a moment and then started to act. He ran to the bathroom and made a tourniquet and some bandages out of torn towel strips. He kept looking at the door. No-one seemed to have heard anything yet. Or if they had, they had no reason to assume that two bangs meant an American mobster had just shot two thugs from England in the middle of the season. Two bangs could mean anything. A party of Mexicans celebrating the Day of the Dead. Or just another failed suicide attempt. But he couldn't stay here now. He undressed and then bandaged and tied up his leg. After putting his pants back on he put the gun back in his waistband. His trousers were covered in blood, but they were black. And the slit where the knife had gone into the cloth was not visible. It wouldn't be too obvious unless someone examined him. He could have spilled coffee on them.

He stumbled out of the hotel. There was a taxi rank outside. At first the taxi driver didn't want to take him. Garner gave him all the notes he had left in his pocket up front. He was in no position to walk. It wasn't until he was halfway to the Tivoli that he realised he had left his wallet in the bedside drawer. The money in his pocket had been enough for the fare, but he could never go back to the hotel with two dead bodies in it. He was broke, cleaned out. £8200 drained away to nothing. His body was broken to bits. He staggered on, breathing heavily and whimpering alternately.

It was at this moment, that Garner had a crazed epiphany. *He* was the strongest. He had pushed and shoved and forced his way here, ahead of everyone else. He deserved the spoils because he had not given up. His stubborn perseverance had paid off. He had borne the buffetings, barbs and blows of his opponents with Stoic pride. The reward was his because he was the strongest. That photo was his title deed.

The taxi dropped him off at the Tivoli Variety Theatre and he managed to find the stage door. He walked in. It was full of bustle. A lot of people busy getting a show together were milling about. He could have been anyone and there was nothing about him to suggest he had no business being there. The place was too big for security. A lot of places are. There isn't enough security in the world to make everywhere safe, not when the world is growing full of malice. People were coming and going in profusion. Some of them were dressed in very odd stage costumes. No-one would have noticed a pantomime horse in amongst this carnival. Garner felt as though he were in Rio de Janeiro. If anyone challenged him, he would say, 'I'm the sword-swallower. I've had an accident'.

CHAPTER TWENTY-SEVEN

He moved upstairs towards the dressing rooms. He had one hand on the gun in his jacket pocket. No-one stopped him or asked who he was. These were innocent times. But they were also the end of innocent times.

Garner burst into a room at the end of a corridor and closed the door behind himself. The room itself was clearly a star's dressing room. It was spacious and luxurious. There was a velvet banquette along one wall and counters for make-up with mirrors. Standing in front of him, as if in an illusion caused by his illness, was Marlene Dietrich. She was obviously in the middle of changing and was wearing a golden shimmering dressing gown. Even in his painful and broken state, Garner could not fail to register the extraordinary sexual charisma of the greatest star in all of show business, now in her 60s but still glistening with allure. She was holding - of all damn things – a packet of Ajax, and appeared to be in the process of cleaning down her make-up counter. But it didn't make her any less refulgent.

In those days, a star was still a star. Nowadays you can be the star of a television commercial. You can be a star if you are a bit part in a soap opera. These days a newsreader is a star. Marlene Dietrich was probably the last real one: a blazing, heavenly entity with the power to spellbind everyone in the audience – male and female – no matter what the size of the theatre. And every one of them would think that she was singing just to them. Truthfully, she could never sing or act very well, but her hypnotized adulators never noticed.

In the middle of the room was a coffee table with two chairs. Garner slumped into one of them, pointing his gun at Miss Dietrich who registered zero fear or concern. She simply said,

'Who are you? What do you want? This is my dressing room. How dare you come in here. Would you get out, please.'

And then Garner noticed someone else in the room. Sitting cross-legged on the counter behind him was the blonde woman. She was dressed in a basque and fishnet tights but with a split maxi skirt attached by a clasp to make the ensemble look like an evening gown. She had been filing her nails when he entered. But now she was looking at him. Garner jerked his gun towards the great star and said,

'This is loaded. Don't think I won't use it.'

'I certainly won't,' she purred calmly. 'A man like you would always use a gun. It is the only thing he has. Without the gun, you are nothing. It is all that stands between you and obscurity.'

'Quiet,' said Garner. 'I'm sick to my stomach of everyone's repartee. I want the box and I'm not leaving without it.'

Then he looked behind himself.

'You, Blondie, get over here where I can see you.'

It was his last and most terrible error. The blonde woman slipped lightly off the counter and walked behind him. He let her do it. What happened next was one of those unbelievable moments where reason is suspended and the mind is thrown into complete confusion as it struggles to comprehend what cannot be comprehended, what is against all the laws of science and logic.

Suddenly, an incredible and irresistible power forced his arm upwards. No matter how much he tried to regain control of it, it stayed there as though it were manacled to the ceiling. At the same time, a similar force took hold around his throat and neck. He was pushed down and his head hit the table. He struggled like a maniac, trying to push his body upwards, but whoever was behind him was effortlessly far stronger than he. The door was closed and had locked itself. Had some terrible classical genie walked through the wall? Had an enormous wrestler emerged from the wardrobe? But he couldn't smell any sulphur or testosterone or wrestler's perspiration. Just the smell of perfume. It wasn't Marlene's perfume at $500 a teardrop. It was perfume bought from the counter at Boots. (Garner had known enough women to know what cheap perfume smelled like.)

'I would advise you to stop struggling,' said Marlene. 'Miss Rhodes is very strong. She could easily break your neck.'

The blonde woman spoke for the first time. She had an almost comically exaggerated upper-class English accent, the sort which often betrays low origins. It is called a 'cut-glass' accent in England.

'I don't even want to break his wrist. I don't wish to hurt him at all. Now whoever you are, will you please drop that silly pistol?'

Garner didn't know where to hurt first. His jaw was in agony, pressed against the table. His kidneys were screaming again. His leg was throbbing. The tourniquet was cutting into his thigh. And his wrist was about to break as the strong lady twisted it back and pushed his neck downwards. But he wouldn't let go. Marlene came closer to him and bent down to speak.

'Drop it you stupid, stubborn man. The game is over, whatever your game is. It's all over. You are finished. It's too late to fight now.'

She stepped back to look at him with penetrating knowledge. Then she added, 'It was probably always too late with you.'

But Garner wouldn't drop the gun and it had to be twisted out of his grasp. The pain was unbearable, and the gun eventually fell. Marlene gracefully picked it up and pointed it at him.

'You can stop now, Joan. I think he's had enough. Stand back quickly: he may try to lunge at you.'

Joan stood back and then moved round to Marlene's side. But Garner was not in any lunging mood. He started to cry, weeping at first and then sobbing. And finally, a terrible howling of despair and defeat. His body began to jerk with profound spasms, which must have made his wounds even more painful. Then he collapsed onto the floor, sobbing and bawling like an abandoned child. He was, as the Bible would say, broken beyond healing.

Joan looked at Marlene in bewilderment. The sobbing man was crying, 'Mama! Oh, Mama!' Then she knelt down beside him. She looked again at Marlene. Then she tenderly lifted up Garner's 190lb frame as if he were a baby and placed it on the banquette. Garner just kept on bawling. And the two ladies just stared at him and at each other. Someone was banging on the dressing room door.

CHAPTER TWENTY-EIGHT

It had been a good day out for the locals of South London. The Five Star Gym had hosted a celebrity and sporting event for charity. Although the purpose was to raise money for a local children's unit at the hospital, the theme had been light-hearted.
There was comedy wrestling – not much less convincing than the real thing – from Pallo and McManus, as well as a comic weightlifting competition.
Freddie Mills was the master of ceremonies, flexing his muscles and clowning around. The barbell in the middle of the floor weighed 360lbs. A forgotten music hall comic called Charlie Chips had made a good routine out of trying to lift it and inflicting pretended injuries upon himself. Diana Dors dropped in to help out and be photographed.
There were less reputable characters present too. There were a couple of the local hard boys who had learned from the Kray brothers that charity events could be good publicity and cost nothing. Also present was DJ Jimmy Savile, learning his profession of making money out of other people's infirmities. Like some ghastly little Rumpelstiltskin, he was developing the ability to spin the coarse yarn of ordinary people's good intentions into soiled lucre.
'Well, well,' said Mills, who held the compere's microphone. 'Looks like nobody can lift the barbell. Is there nobody in my kingdom who can lift this weight? Surely somebody can lift it? Nobody?'
He bent down to talk to a young boy.
'Do you think you could lift it?'

The boy shook his head.

'Well, I bet I know someone who can.'

He turned to the blonde lady holding the big cardboard cheque.

'At the moment she's holding 125 pounds, but she can lift a lot more than that. Come on, Joanie,' said Freddie. 'Show us how it's done. Give a big hand for The Mighty Mannequin herself! Ladies and Gentlemen, Miss Joan Rhodes!'

There was a round of applause. The blonde woman put down the cardboard cheque and moved behind the barbell. There was a hush – more bewildered than expectant. Some knew her from the cinema and television. Others didn't, as she was never greatly famous and few of them would have had televisions. Was she another comedy turn? She grabbed the barbell purposefully and jerked it, first up to her chest and then above her head. No man present could have come near to the feat.

The round of applause was less than you might think. Many were simply stunned.

'It's a trick,' said someone. A lot could not believe it. How could there be such titanic strength in that slender and elegant body? But it was no trick. She dropped the barbell with a huge crash that so testified.

She posed for the camera, lifting both Mills and Pallo off the ground, one in each arm. There were a few reporters there from local rags and agencies. But all they wanted was pictures of Diana Dors.

CHAPTER TWENTY-NINE

The urgent knocking on the dressing room door continued.
'*Hvad er der galt*? Anything wrong, Miss Dietrich?' shouted the stage manager. He tried to open the door, but it had self-locked from the inside. Marlene hid the gun in a drawer and then opened the door a little so that the man could not enter.
'No Pieter. Thank you. Everything is fine. There is nothing to see here.'
'I thought I heard someone shouting. The strong lady is due on stage in two minutes.'
'She will be there.'
Suddenly, Garner heaved himself up and barged Marlene and the stage manager out of the way. He ran out the way he came in, down the stairs, banging against walls and whimpering with pain. He ran awkwardly out of the stage door and into the street. He must have presented quite a spectacle since he was still howling and bawling like a lost soul. He disappeared into the milling summer crowds. He was never seen alive again by anyone who knew him.
A week or so later, they fished his body out of the Rhine. His shoes were in a terrible state. The West German investigating officer speculated that he might have been trying to walk home. How he proposed to negotiate the English Channel was anyone's guess, he said. He seemed to be impressed that a man had gotten so far with an injured leg and a broken jaw. It was also clear from the examination that some great force – obviously a very large man - had wrenched the muscles of his wrist and may have tried to strangle him. There was a

considerable deal of speculation about how he had managed to reach West Germany. Perhaps he had hitch-hiked part of the way - although this was unlikely, given the state he was in. He may have jumped a lorry. Or he may have just walked, as the state of his feet testified. His verdict was that Mr Garner was 'clearly a man of some determination, if not high intelligence'. He had no more than a few Danish krone but was carrying a list of names and bank account numbers. The West German police said they would be happy to restore the list to its rightful owner. Nobody came forward. And with the unclaimed list in the safekeeping of the authorities, the second list became worthless.

When Diana Dors heard the story of his journey home, she is said to have commented, 'He seems to have been going in the right direction. That's a first.'

His funeral would have been a cheap affair at the expense of the public in Germany. Ruby would probably not have gone, even if she had been able to afford to. Her parents had stood by her as a single mother, but it may have been part of the price that she wash her hands of any memory of Garner. Madge, her mother, might have been worried about what the neighbours would say. She was relieved and pleasantly surprised at their offers of help and expressions of sympathy. Just when you're prepared to think the worst of people, others restore your faith.

Tommy received a suspended sentence for his brief foray into breaking and entering; but he was more chastened by the revelation of Garner's behaviour towards his sister. The judge was impressed with the extent to which he had co-operated with the police.

A few months later, a woman turned up in Chicago, claiming to be Garner's wife. She asked if there was any money, and on being told that there was none, went away again. Clearly, she had not known him that well, but she may have figured that there was a chance. He may have convinced her that he was lucky or was about to be lucky or was expecting some luck. Garner had that effect on some people.

CHAPTER THIRTY

Copenhagen is held out at arm's length to the East by the jutting peninsula which is Denmark. The city lies within a mesh of canals and sea straits which form the uncertain boundary between her and Sweden. In the summer it is delightful and there are wonderful sea breezes moving across the whole complex. These breezes ruffled the flimsy summer frocks of Marlene Dietrich and Joan Rhodes as they strolled arm-in-arm along the Nyhavn Canal, admiring the pretty multi-coloured houses that lined the way. It was the last day of their little adventure together and they were both a little sad. Marlene had finished her two-week run in Copenhagen and was soon to return home. Joan had been asked to stay on and support Shirley Bassey.

Marlene was disguised by a headscarf and dark glasses. The legendary actress and the glamorous Titan looked like two ordinary women out for a stroll in the sun. Not that the unexcitable Danes would have cared anyway.

Marlene bought her an ice cream. This was surreal, thought Joan. Born into poverty and sent to the workhouse - and Marlene Dietrich was buying her an ice cream.

'I must be careful with sugar or I'll start to look like a real strongwoman. I mean like everyone's idea of one. Perhaps then they'll take me seriously.'

They stopped to admire themselves on a poster advertising the show.

'Do you know, Marlene,' said Joan, 'when they booked me to play in Copenhagen, I knew that you were performing here but I didn't know I was on the same bill until I saw the posters? I saw them from the taxi on the way from the airport. I shouted at him to stop as if he wouldn't understand, but he spoke better English than I did.'

She stopped talking suddenly, aware of her fluttering and endless chatter. The older woman smiled.

'I hope you were pleasantly surprised, my dear.'

'Surprised isn't the word. I was thrilled. And now walking along the waterfront with you, having lunch with you… it's all too much.'

'But you have played with other famous people. You told me you played in front of the Queen.'

'Yes, I went to the Palace one Christmas to perform. Her Majesty was very sweet, but she didn't buy me an ice cream.'

They both smiled again.

'And others?'

'Yes, I've played with many stars. In 1955, I performed with Bob Hope. I dropped him on his head. It makes it sound as though he was too heavy but he was a bag of feathers really. I just lost my balance. I think it ruined my chances of breaking into the American market. There's always something. Some malicious star that drags me down again, that consigns me to obscurity. It's strange, isn't it? Some people rise effortlessly and others can't pick themselves up from the ground. As if it's all ordained somehow. But you're the most special person I ever met, Marlene. Truly, you're the dream come true.'

She stopped so she could say this directly to the German star's face. Marlene took off her dark glasses.

'Nonsense. Look at me. I'm just an old film star trying to make a living. One day, you and I both will be forgotten.'

They walked on again.

'I'm hardly remembered now,' said Joan. There was a pause and then she said, 'The woman who dropped Bob Hope. That's how they'll remember me. If they remember me.'

'If they remember Bob Hope,' said Marlene.

'And what about you? What will you be remembered for?'

'I shall be that woman who kept going long after she should have retired. I'll still be performing after I've been forgotten. Now that will be an achievement. Perhaps it isn't a virtue to keep going. You have to know when to stop in life.'

'I'm stubborn,' said Joan. 'I know one day I will keep going long after my strength has faded. One day when I'm old I won't be able to *lift* a telephone directory, never mind tear it in half. And then I'll be ordinary again, thank God. But I will have touched the Moon.'

'Others may forget us, but we will have our memories,' said the actress.

'They will never forget you, I'm sure of that, Marlene.'

'They will forget. And a good thing too. No-one wants to be immortal. At least not in this life. Living until ninety is bad enough. Life is such a bore.'

They made their way towards their favourite seafood restaurant at the Fisherman's Wharf.

'When did you first find out?' asked Marlene suddenly.

'About what?...Oh that. You know it's funny...you don't really find out that you've *got* something special; you find out that other people don't.'

Marlene nodded. She understood.

'I was eleven years old, in my auntie's pub. Just a little girl. I used to watch the men rolling in the firkins of ale. They weigh about a hundred and twelve pounds...'

She paused. She felt she was being boring, but Marlene seemed rapt. Such a legend and she was listening to her blathering on about barrels of ale in a London pub.

'Please go on. This is fascinating.'

'Well, one day I asked them why they rolled them. Why didn't they carry them? "Oh, bless you, young Miss, they're far too heavy for that."' So, I said, "Well, I can carry one."'

'And they told you that only naughty little girls told stories.'

'Something like that, yes.'

'And then you lifted one up for them.'

Joan paused in her walk and looked sadly out across the water, idly licking her cornet. She had the oddest face. When she was smiling, it was radiant. But when she was not smiling her face seemed to invert, as if her two expressions were the masks of classical Greek drama. You could see all the pain when she wasn't hiding it.

'And you'll never forget the look on their faces.'

'Yes. That's when I knew I was a...'

'Don't say that! Don't you ever say that! You are beautiful! You are magnificent.'

'No, Marlene; *you* are magnificent. I just bend steel bars in my teeth and tear up telephone directories. It really is the most bizarre way to make a living.'

Marlene stopped again to caress Joan's hair, putting it back in place after the breeze had disarranged it.

'Now, Joan, before we part, will you tell me what he wanted?'

'What makes you think I know?'

'I know. I mean I know that you know.'

Joan reached into her voluminous shoulder bag and drew out a curious wooden box, made of slats of wood, all different shades of brown.

'This, probably. Freddie Mills gave it to me. I saw him a week after we'd appeared together at a charity do at this gym I go to. It was a present for helping out at the function. He knew I wouldn't take any expenses, but he wanted to give me something. He joked that he wanted my autograph, so I signed the newspaper photo *To the strongest the spoils*! The box was one of two. I think he must have given me the wrong one. I'll never know if he gave it to me accidentally or deliberately. He might just have wanted to hide it somewhere.'

'That was dangerous for you.'

'Then I don't think he did it deliberately. I want to believe that.'

'But you can't be sure.'

Marlene took the box and tapped it on the waterfront railing.

'It is very robust. Looks as though it is made of teak. Do you know how to open it?'

'Oh, yes,' said Joan. 'I have a special method.'

She took back the box and placed it in her palm. She looked at it fondly for a moment and then closed her elegant iron hand, crushing the box into a hundred bits of matchwood. Inside was a piece of paper. Marlene picked it out and looked at it in mystification. It was a typed list of bank names and surnames. Then she returned it to Joan.

'What is it?'

'Something evil,' said Joan, after a pause. 'Something nobody should have.' She screwed up the piece of paper and threw it into the water.

'"Men and bits of paper, blown by a cold wind," - T S Eliot,' said the actress. And then after a pause, she said, 'Why did this man Mills have it?'

'Why? I don't know. Think of a game of pass the parcel played by overgrown children. Criminals, celebrities and sportsmen. Everything is blurred by drink and the whirl of the party. Good people find the company of bad people glamorous and exciting. Everything is so much fun until someone gets killed or jailed. People supping with the devil and using very short spoons.'

'Yes, I know that feeling. They love the sense of danger until things get dangerous. Then they want to run home to mother. Why did he want it?'

'He probably thought it gave him a line of credit. I don't know. I'm guessing. I don't think I want to know.'

Marlene reached into her own bag. She drew out something heavy wrapped in a scarf. She waited until they were between two canal boats. Then she knelt down and dropped the package surreptitiously into the water.

'And we commit them to the sea.'

'Amen,' said Joan.

'Oh, but your poor little hand. You may have splinters,' said Marlene as she took Joan's hand and dabbed it lovingly with her handkerchief, smiling at her all the while.

Then she winked and said, 'You and I are good at keeping secrets, I think.'

EPILOGUE

Garner thought he was a gambler. But he really wasn't. In a sense, there is no such thing as gambling. It can't exist because the House always wins over the long term – and gambling can never be a short-term vice.

If the House always wins, then gambling is an illusion, supported and obscured by the pagan rituals of crossed fingers, bated breath and whispered prayers to the false gods of Fortune and Freedom of Choice. Perhaps Garner was born for the German river. There is no rule that says a man's destiny has to be dignified. It took him a long time to get there but his rendezvous was never in doubt - and the path to any river is always downwards. Perhaps it would have been some comfort to know that despite his stumbles, deviations, missteps and mistakes, he was always going in the right direction.

On July 25th, 1965, Freddie Mills was found shot to death in his own car round the back of his Soho nightclub. The official verdict was suicide, which was hotly disputed by his family. There were stories of protection money not paid and gangster threats. There was one mooted hypothesis that Mills had tried to use some kind of information about criminal activity to prise money out of his underworld contacts. The truth may never be known and as usual, as with the Kennedy assassination and other mysteries, the more speculation and investigation there is, the bigger the pile of muck that obscures the truth. Mills' association with known criminals like the Kray Brothers has fuelled the speculation.

The Kray Brothers. Particularly vicious gangsters. Twin brothers who ran organised crime in the East End of London. They were considered celebrities at one time and had many friends in show business, politics and the sporting world. They were once photographed by the celebrated photographer David Bailey.

Diana Dors, actress, lived only to be 53. Her career, which was in the doldrums in the sixties, revived later on, on British television. Afflicted by cancer but comforted by her faith in God, she died in 1984. At her funeral there was a giant floral tribute from the Kray Brothers.

Barbara Windsor remained famous and a national treasure for most of her life. She was created a Dame Commander in 2016 and died in 2020, aged 83. Both she and Dors were friends and associates of the Kray Twins.

Ronnie Knight, who divorced Windsor in 1985, received seven years in prison in 1995 for handling stolen money. As of writing, he is still alive.

Marlene Dietrich, the legendary actress, who needs no biographical note, became a recluse in Paris in her 80s. Her great beauty gone, she was said to be afraid to look at herself in the mirror. She died in 1992, aged 91.

Joan Rhodes a.k.a. The Mighty Mannequin, model and variety artiste, performed as a strongwoman for thirty-five years. Despite being a svelte and attractive 135lbs, she was able to lift a 180lb blacksmith's anvil with one hand. She began to lose her superhuman strength in her mid-50s. After failing to break into acting, she opened a café in Crouch End, London. She knew many people in the sporting and entertainment world, including Freddie Mills and Jackie Pallo. She was a friend of

Quentin Crisp for fifty years. She died in 2010, aged 89. Unlike the other names in this list, she has been completely forgotten. This obscurity is as inexplicable as the mystery of her incredible strength.

Freddie Foreman, gangster in the South of London area. He was a friend of Detective Inspector Frank Williams, an association which caused much concern. Foreman is still alive at the time of writing, aged 90 and suffering from illness.

Detective Inspector Frank Williams. Former commando and war hero in Italy during the war. Deputy to Tommy Butler of the Flying Squad during the Great Train Robbery investigation. He knew more about the London underworld than any policeman because of his controversial association with known criminals.

Jimmy Savile. BBC presenter. Savile was a disc jockey who used charitable activities to gain publicity and make his fortune. He also used his influence to seduce or molest underage girls. The BBC, normally a ruthless and hypercritical judge of other peoples' infractions, covered up his crimes, which were not fully revealed until after Savile's death.

On July 8th, while Marlene Dietrich and Joan Rhodes were in Copenhagen, Ronald Biggs the Train Robber escaped from prison. This proved to some that there were still influential elements involved in the robbery who were still at large. Stories about a Mr Big were revived and added to, although truthfully Biggs had been a minor player in the heist. Biggs escaped eventually to Brazil, where he became something of a folk hero. But the money had run out long before Biggs was forgotten.

The Great Train Robbery in 1963 had been an important watershed in British Life. The immediate post war period was seen by some as a time of innocence. Naivety, said others, if not complacency. The robbery represented something far more significant than just the theft of a large amount of money. It was an attack upon the self-regard of society. It was presumed that no-one would touch the money made sacred by its association with the Royal Mail. And if these days there is stricter security at your average cake-shop than there was at your average bank in the fifties, it is largely because of the robbery itself.

Many ordinary British people admitted that they sympathised with this daring crime and wished well to the ones who escaped. Their sentences of thirty years in some cases were said to have caused outrage – although it seems to have been forgotten that they barely served more than a third of that time. The robbers became celebrities – some even secured book deals. But most were pursued by retribution of various kinds.

This robbery was the first of many taboos to come crashing down, under assault from literature, entertainment, theatre, the music industry, political agitation and the glamorisation of vice by the popular media. Those taboos are still coming down today, although truthfully there cannot be many left. Civilisation cannot exist without taboos. There must always be dark and fearful places where people do not dare to go. If not, then everywhere is doomed to become dark and fearful.

Some people think that society is getting better, going upwards, progressing. Such people cannot be reasoned with because they are mad. Humanity does not progress or evolve. It stumbles and crashes blindly forward, reaching wildly, eyes always into the sun, cascading downwards. And at the bottom of the valleys, waiting unseen like dark snakes, are the rivers that consume us.

Printed in Great Britain
by Amazon